THOSE FOUR
AND PLENTY MORE

Eleanor Curtis Dewees

THOSE FOUR
AND PLENTY MORE

REVIEW AND HERALD PUBLISHING ASSOCIATION
Washington, D.C. 20012

Editor: Bobbie Jane Van Dolson

Book Design: Alan Forquer
Cover Illustration: Warren Rood

Printed in U.S.A.

Library of Congress Catalog Card No. 81-10554
ISBN 0-8280-0092-1

CONTENTS

OLD
CROOK

THE WILLIAMS FAMILY
lived in Burlington right alongside the railroad tracks. The train stopped
each day right there at the platform beside the Williams place. Anyone
wanting to travel somewhere could walk over to the platform, and sure
enough, the train would stop and pick him up.

Now, that wasn't the only wonderful thing about the Williams
family. Oh, no, indeed! The best part was the people. You guessed that,
of course, didn't you?

First there was Mr. Williams. Besides being the father, he was the
oldest and the tallest and the biggest. Yes, and the kindest, most
wonderful father in the world. Just ask any of the Williams children and
they will tell you that was so. Mr. Williams had dark reddish hair. It was
wavy, almost curly. He had a prickly, handsome mustache that just
matched his hair except that it wasn't wavy. And he had hazel eyes.
Hazel eyes are very interesting, you know. Sometimes they look blue,
sometimes they look gray, sometimes they look brown, and sometimes
you are just sure that they are green, just plain green. Mr. Williams had
an interesting nose, too. It was bumpy. Auntie said that it looked like a
pump handle. Then Daddy Williams would tell her that *hers* looked like
a scythe hanging over the fence. Mrs. Williams, the mother of the
family, said that it was Daddy's nose that made him so handsome, and
he seemed pleased with that. Oh, yes, Mr. Williams' other name was
Daddy. Every one of the Williamses called him that, even Mrs.
Williams.

Mrs. Williams, or Mommy, was a pretty woman. Pretty? No, she
was *beautiful*. She wasn't nearly as tall as Mr. Williams. She had lots

and lots of dark-brown hair that she piled in fluffs and swirls around her head. Her hair was so long that she could almost sit on it. Her eyebrows were dark, too, and so were her eyelashes; and her eyes were the deepest, darkest, loveliest blue you ever saw. She had very white skin. She was simply altogether lovely. Just ask anyone.

Then there were the Williams children. Mr. Williams would just shake his head when he looked at his large family. He said that their household was like that of the old woman who lived in a shoe, who had so many children she didn't know what to do. Mrs. Williams said that that wasn't so at all. She had a lot of children, it was true, but *she* knew *exactly* what to do. Why, that was simple. On Mondays she hauled out the washtubs, got the old scrubbing board, a couple of bars of strong yellow soap, and her bluing bottle, and went to work. On Tuesdays she put all the sadirons on the stove to heat, set her ironing board over the backs of two chairs, brought out the baskets of clean clothes, and got busy. The rest of the time she mended clothes, sewed clothes, cooked meals, cleaned house, made bread, cookies, cakes, rolls, and all kinds of things. She canned fruit, mended toys, took care of such things as sniffles, earaches, bumps, and bruises. She even embroidered things and crocheted things. Yes, unlike the old woman in the shoe, she knew just what to do, and that was to keep busy.

About all those children. Norine was the oldest. She was a pretty little girl with large blue eyes and soft, silky, golden-blond hair. She was so smart! She could read books before she ever started to school.

The next child was Jessie. Jessie looked a lot like her daddy because she had dark reddish hair too, but it was terribly straight. She had freckles and hazel eyes. She liked to play and get into mischief, climb fences, and do things like that.

Ilene, a year younger than Jessie, was the third little girl. She was very quiet and very good and obedient. She wasn't at all like Jessie, though the two were the best of friends and hardly ever quarreled unless Jessie started it. Ilene had big blue eyes and pale-blond hair. Yes, she was pretty special.

The last little girl was Midget. Midget? What a funny name! Well, that wasn't exactly her real name. Not the name she got before she was even born. No, not exactly. Before she was born Daddy wanted her named Mary or Martha, but when this poor little Mary-Martha was born she weighed barely four pounds, so Daddy right away began calling her Midget. And that is what people called her ever after.

No family should have all girls, should it? The Williams family didn't have all girls either. They had Sonny. Oh, that wasn't his real name either. His real name was Henry, but the first boy after four girls should naturally be called Sonny, don't you think? So that was his name. Sonny was the baby and didn't play with the girls.

Daddy Williams had built a swing for the girls, and he had hung a hammock in the front yard between the two big maple trees. The hammock was made out of gunnysacks and was just about the nicest place to play in the world. Almost the nicest, but not quite.

Some days in Burlington were warm and sticky. Oh, more than that, they were dreadfully hot. Too hot to play outside, too hot to play inside, too hot to do anything at all. It would have been just awful if it weren't for one thing. That one big grand thing—the basement!

Oh, yes, the Williams girls had a basement in their large home. Well, maybe not a basement like you and I have in our homes, with switch-on lights and a neat cement floor, with rows and rows of shelves for fruit or vegetables and sometimes jams and jellies. Nor did it have tools and workbenches and saws and gadgets. Nor was it a basement with an electric train and a rumpus room with a fireplace in it, like some people have. No, it wasn't like any of those. This basement had a cool, hard-packed dirt floor. It was all open on one end, but didn't have so much as a window on the other three sides. Yes, maybe it was a little bit dark and spooky, particularly way at the back, but one would have to crawl on his hands and knees to get there, and there wasn't one thing at the back anyway. So nobody went there.

The basement had a few things in it. A pile of odds and ends of lumber was stacked against one wall. It might have been fun to play with that lumber if it hadn't been for something else. And that something else was what made playing in the basement so much fun. You could never guess what it was. No, you could never guess. Well, there, stacked against one wall stood a bunch of old, discarded window shades. You don't know what they are? No, of course you don't. You have probably never seen dark-green window shades. You probably even wonder what could have been so much fun about them, whatever they were. Well, dark-green window shades almost made the most wonderful chalkboards in the world. And if you have chalkboards, you can play school, can't you? And if you don't like to play school, that is because you have never played that game in a big, cool basement on a dreadfully sticky, hot day with Norine as the teacher. Norine could read, you know. And she could do numbers and write and draw and sing. Yes, she knew lots of songs from school, and she taught them to her little students. They could draw pictures on the old dark-green blinds, and Norine would help them. They could all write numbers and letters on those old shades, and Norine would help them with that, too.

Yes, Norine was the teacher. Jessie, Ilene, Midget, and some of the neighborhood children were the students. Delores and Dorothy and Faye brought their dollies, so there really was quite a big school in that cool basement on a dreadfully hot, sticky day.

Old Crook came to school too. Class would just nicely get started when Old Crook would saunter into the schoolroom, tardy as usual. He would peer around, green eyes large in the semidarkness, and then when he had everyone's attention he would stroll leisurely over to the teacher, kiss her briefly on the cheek, then sprawl at her feet. He paid absolutely no attention to anything she might be teaching at the time. No, indeed. In fact, he just lay there, eyes half closed, indifferent to everything and everyone. There was no question but that he was teacher's pet. No question at all. Norine would quite likely reach over and draw him a bit closer to her side. Sometimes he was so bold that he might even take the liberty of climbing onto her lap. But that was Old Crook's way, and no one seemed to mind at all. Who was Old Crook? Where did he come from?

Well, Old Crook just wandered into the Williams household one day. Someone stooped to pet him, Norine got him a saucer of milk, and he decided to stay right there forever. Right then and there Old Crook adopted Norine or she adopted him, or something like that. Of course, he loved all the Williams children. And they all loved him. He was their cat, and no cat was quite so wonderful as Old Crook. Yes, he was wonderful. Not that he was so beautiful to look at, but he had his own definite marking that made him different from all other cats anywhere. And to make him even more special he had a definite crook in his tail! Usually his long tail hung almost straight down or it stood almost straight up, depending on his mood. Almost straight, that is, but not quite. About an inch from the end that tail quit hanging straight up or straight down and turned at a definite right angle, and the tip of his tail always pointed to the left, even when he was a little bit angry and swished it back and forth.

Where had Old Crook gotten his unusual tail? Well, no one seemed to know for sure. Maybe someone had slammed the door shut when he was almost outside the house or else almost inside the house. Anyway, he was a marked cat, but he didn't mind. He soon found that his poor broken tail made the Williams family and even the neighbors love him all the more. All the children petted him and crooned over him and talked to him about his crooked tail.

When Old Crook roamed around the neighborhood, which he enjoyed doing, he wasn't always recognized by his meow or his purr. All cats sound pretty much alike when they meow or purr, particularly alley cats. And there were many other cats that looked almost like Old Crook—but not exactly, because of that special crooked tail. He could get attention and sympathy at any neighborhood house by meowing pitifully. He would be identified immediately as poor Old Crook. Then he would be petted and talked to and fed. No broom was swished at him. Oh, no! After plenty of loving care Old Crook was picked up tenderly, although sometimes ungracefully, and lugged back home. Sometimes he disliked these tender attentions. After all, if you were a cat, do you think you would enjoy being grasped firmly about the middle, two feet and a tail drooping down one side and two feet and your head dangling down the other side? But Old Crook was tolerant and kind, and he would rumble his thanks.

Oh, Old Crook really loved his family, no doubt of that. And they were very good to him. He surely couldn't complain a bit about their treatment. Of course, Daddy Williams often said that he had absolutely no use for alley cats, particularly stray ones that bummed the neighborhood. But Old Crook and Daddy Williams knew something that Mommy and the children never knew. Yes, Old Crook and Daddy had their own particular secret. You see, every once in a while when no one, positively *no one,* was looking, Daddy would stoop over and give Old Crook some tender loving and petting too. But that was their secret—just Old Crook's and Daddy's.

The one thing that really bothered Old Crook was the grown-ups' attitude about his sleeping upstairs with the girls. Daddy and Mommy had this funny idea about cats having to be outside at night. They kept trying to explain to the girls that cats liked to hunt at night. The girls never really accepted that idea, nor did Old Crook. Maybe it was his age, but he knew that if he had been asked, he would have admitted liking to sleep at the foot of a nice soft bed rather than being turned outside in all kinds of weather and other discomforts such as fighting beasts. But no one consulted him, nor did they take into consideration any of the arguments and pleadings of those beautiful girls. So promptly at bedtime each evening Old Crook was escorted with deep apologies to the back door to begin his lonely nighttime wanderings.

Sometimes this clever cat escaped the usual dumping-outside-of-the-house process. It took quick action, no one could deny that. He was pushed outside the door, but before the door could slam shut he sometimes managed to scoot back inside. At great risk to his injured tail, naturally. At such times he would stay hidden in the shadows until the door to the stairs would be left open. Then he would pad quietly up the bedroom steps and crouch in the shadows until the girls came up to their beds. When the lamp had been blown out and all four little girls gathered around Norine's bed to say their prayers, Old Crook would jump into their midst. When the girls came to the ''God bless'' part of their prayers and they had prayed for God's blessings on Daddy and Mommy and Sonny and Aunt Rose Ann and Uncle Dow and lots of other people, then it was that several little hands would reach out to that special furry bundle in their midst, and as they gently stroked Old Crook's head and back, some little voice would pray, ''And please bless Old Crook, too.'' Old Crook would rumble his Amen right along with the girls, and they would all climb into their beds, Norine and Jessie in one, Ilene and Midget in another. Old Crook usually settled down at Norine's feet, his head tucked under his paws, his legs and body curled around his head, and that long bent tail circling everything.

Mother or Daddy sometimes found Old Crook happily asleep with his favorite people, and would smile. Don't you suppose Jesus looked down and smiled too? Don't you think He loves cats? After all, He did make them even before He made people, didn't He?

GUESS WHAT!

NORINE, WOULD YOU LIKE to come to my house to see my brand-new surprise?''

A surprise! Well, what would you say if someone talked to you like that? Wouldn't you like to see a brand-new surprise? Of course you would. All boys and girls like surprises, and Norine did too. She was interested right away.

"What is it, Jackie?"

"Oh, I can't tell you or it won't be a surprise. Wouldn't you like to see it? It's the best surprise in the world! You'll like it, Norine. Honest you will. Come on. It's over at my house. *Come on,* Norine. Please hurry!"

But Norine didn't hurry. Why? Didn't she like surprises? Of course she did. She liked them just as you do. Yes, every bit as much, but she was making a surprise of her own, a picture for her mother. She sat there humped over her school desk, curly golden hair around her face, carefully outlining a picture of the big white house with the high steps up the back and the two big maples with the hammock in the front yard. She had to add some flowers around the house, too, because Mother always had lots of flowers growing. Then she drew four little girls and Mommy and Daddy. And she mustn't forget Sonny, the baby. She put him in Daddy's arms. There, it was finished. Norine leaned back and looked at her picture, and said with a pleased sigh, "That's a real good picture, isn't it, Jackie?"

Jackie stood beside Norine's desk, smiling at her. His eyes squinted almost shut when he smiled. Freckles trailed across his nose and cheeks, and neatly combed corn-silk hair framed his chubby face. He and Norine were both first-graders and were the very best of friends. Now Jackie repeated his question, "Wouldn't you like to see my surprise, Norine? Mother says I can show you if you want to come. You do want to come, don't you?" His question was anxious, pleading.

Norine glanced down at her beautiful picture. "Is your surprise as nice as this picture that I'm going to give to my mother?" She just knew nothing could be that nice, of course. And Mother would be so happy.

"My surprise is beautiful. Just wait. You'll see what I mean." Jackie's eyes crinkled in eager expectancy. "Come on, Norine! Let's hurry."

"We will have to go around my place first because I must ask Mommy," Norine reminded Jackie.

"Yes, of course. We'll go by your house, but do please hurry or maybe we won't be able to see it."

Norine stopped right there, right in the hall of the big, almost-empty school building. "What do you mean, Jackie? You have a surprise, but if we don't hurry we maybe can't see it? What kind of surprise can that be? Will it fly away? Is it a bird?" Secretly Norine disliked birds, particularly birds in cages. They always seemed to be flittering and flapping, and most of the time you couldn't get them to sing. But she supposed she would have to go home with Jackie to see the surprise even if it were a bird.

Norine and Jackie walked down the long hall and out into the sunlight. Norine glanced at Jackie. He wasn't saying a word, just walking along with a smile on his face. Well, she just knew she could find out what the surprise was. Jackie couldn't keep a secret. "What is the surprise, Jackie? Please tell me."

"I can't tell you, or it wouldn't be a surprise anymore."

Well, that was true, but Norine was going to guess anyway. "I'll bet it's a wagon," she said.

Jackie just laughed. "You aren't even close!"

"A drum?"

"No, not a drum. You can never guess it, not ever."

"Then I give up!"

"You can't give up because I can't tell you what it is. It's a real surprise!"

Norine guessed everything she could think of, but for each guess

Jackie just shook his head and laughed. "You'll never guess, Norine, never!"

They had reached the Williams house. All of a sudden Norine saw her cat, Old Crook. "Oh, I have it, Jackie! Your surprise is a new cat. Or maybe it's a soft little kitten! Oh, goody!" And she dashed into the house.

"Mommy, Jackie wants me to go over to his house to see his brand-new little pet kitten. May I go, Mommy?" Now you may not believe this, but Norine was so excited about a fluffy little kitten that she forgot all about her own surprise for Mommy.

Mommy looked down at Norine's eager face, then at Jackie. "Do you have a new kitten at your place, Jackie?" she asked.

"Oh, no, ma'am, not a kitten. It's something else. A real surprise."

"Not a kitten? Well, let's see, maybe I can guess . . . Is it tiny, and kind of soft and nice?"

"Oh, please, ma'am, don't guess! It's little and soft, and, oh, it's the best surprise in the world. Don't tell. I want to surprise Norine! May she come with me?" Jackie sort of danced on one foot and then on the other, jiggling with excitement.

Norine looked at Mommy and then at Jackie. They stood there smiling at each other just as though they both knew a secret. Well, it was probably a puppy. Norine was a little bit disappointed. But she liked puppies better than noisy, twittery birds. Some boys liked turtles and toads and things. Oh, dear! She hoped the surprise wasn't something like that! She shuddered, but when she looked at Jackie's face, she knew it just couldn't be any of those awful things. No, it was probably a puppy. Puppies were nice. Pretty nice, that is, but they liked to jump up on people and lick them in the face and all that.

Norine glanced at Mommy. Mommy was just standing there nodding her head and smiling at Jackie, and he was smiling right back at her. "I think it will be very nice for Norine to go over and see your surprise," she said. And she kept nodding her head in that secret way. After all, everyone likes surprises. Even mommies.

Jackie and Norine trotted off, and before long they were going up the steps to Jackie's house. "We have to be quiet," Jackie whispered. He reached up to the knob of the front door and turned it very, very carefully so it wouldn't make any noise. Both children stepped inside, and Jackie

closed the door behind them very, very softly, hardly making a sound. Then he took Norine's hand and they tiptoed through the living room to the foot of the stairs. Oh, so quietly they walked. "Sh-h-h," Jackie whispered again. "You can't make any noise, not any noise at all. Just follow me."

They mounted the steps slowly. One step, two steps. Norine stepped onto the third step, and, oh, it made a loud creak! Three steps, four steps, and they were on the landing. Norine glanced at Jackie. Excitement brightened his face, but he just placed a finger to his lips, shushing her. But she wasn't going to talk. No, indeed! This was exciting! On up the stairs they went, five steps, six steps, seven, eight, and they were in the upstairs hall. Jackie reached for her hand again, and together they tiptoed into a little room. Jackie led her over to the corner of the room, and there it was!

The surprise was right there in a sort of basket. Yes, there it was! It was nothing but a tiny, red-faced scrap of a baby! What kind of a surprise was that, anyway? Norine knew all about babies. She had been 2 years old when Jessie was born and 3 years old when Ilene was born and 4 years old when Midget was born and past 6 when Sonny was born. Huh! A baby for a surprise! Wordlessly she stared at the wrinkled little creature. She wished it were a kitten or a puppy or anything except just a baby!

Jackie was completely unaware of Norine's disappointment. He just stood gazing at the little bundle. "Isn't she beautiful, Norine?" he whispered. "Isn't she just beautiful?"

Then he lifted his eyes to Norine and said something wonderful. You can't guess what he said, no, not in a million years!

He said, "We named her Norine!"

Well, how about that! Suddenly Norine looked at that surprise and it wasn't just any little, wrinkled, red-faced baby! No, indeed. She was very special and very lovely. And her name was *Norine!*

Yes, Jackie had told the truth. This was the most wonderful surprise in the whole world! A brand-new baby with *her* name—Norine! The disappointment had vanished completely from big Norine's face, and joy had replaced it. She touched one of baby Norine's little soft hands, then smiling, took Jackie's hand, and they tiptoed out, both filled with the pleasure of the most beautiful surprise in the whole world!

Did you know that Jesus has another name? Yes, His other name is Christ. When people love Jesus with all their hearts, they take His other name, Christ, and they are called Christians. How beautiful that name must sound to Jesus when people choose His name because they love Him. Let's take the name Christian because it stands for being kind, loving one another, helping one another, and just being like Jesus. It is such a beautiful name. It will bring us happiness. It will bring other people happiness. And, best of all, when we take that name, Jesus is made very, very happy!

OFF
TO THE
FAIR

COME ON, AUNT INAS. Let's go!" Jessie tugged impatiently at her beloved aunt's hand. Oh, yes, little Jessie was excited, but would you be calm if there were a fair right down the street, just a few blocks away? Oh, no. Not if you were the least little bit like that red-haired Jessie. "Hurry, Aunt Inas. The fair will be all over if we don't go right away," she insisted.

Aunt Inas smiled at her impatient little niece. "Yes, Jessie," she said, "the fair will probably be over before you get all those dirt smudges off your face. And just look at those hands! And your dress! I'm afraid we'll never make it to the fair before it closes." Aunt Inas shook her head sorrowfully.

Jessie looked dismayed. Not make it to the fair? She looked at each hand carefully. Why, they weren't dirty at all. Well-l-l, maybe a little sticky and a tiny little bit grimy. But she wasn't going to miss the fair! No, sirree! She hurried toward the kitchen and the big water pail and the dipper and the washbasin. If Aunt Inas thought she wasn't clean enough to go to the fair, she would just have to get clean enough, that was all.

Aunt Inas, like the good, kind auntie that she was, followed Jessie to the kitchen. "Up you go onto this chair. I have to see what we are doing, and I certainly can't see those ears way down there." Aunt Inas scooped little Jessie up onto a chair, peeled her dress off over her head, and set to work.

"I thought you said my *hands,* Aunt Inas," Jessie managed as the rough, soapy washcloth dug behind her ears and in her ears and under her chin and on the back of her neck. Aunt Inas certainly believed in being clean!

Finally the scrub job was all finished. Aunt Inas pulled a crisp dress over Jessie's head, tied the sash in a pretty bow, brushed Jessie's shiny-red hair, and they were finally ready to go.

"If we hurry, do you think we will get there in time, Aunt Inas?" Jessie worried.

"Oh, yes. I'm sure we'll make it easily and have lots of time to spare. I'm surprised how quickly you got all cleaned up." Aunt Inas spoke admiringly.

A fair is a very exciting place, you know. There are great big cows at fairs. They stand very still, and just keep swishing their tails and moving their jaws around and around and around. They have large eyes and wet noses. There are horses at the fair too. They are something like cows, only taller and scarier. They don't stand still like cows do. Jessie didn't know whether she liked horses or not. If they would only stand still!

At fairs you see rabbits, too. They are so soft, with great tall ears, and they keep wiggling their noses all the time. And, of course, at fairs there are pigs and goats and all kinds of things.

Jessie didn't let Aunt Inas stop long enough to see all she wanted to see or talk to all the people she wanted to talk to. Oh, no! What if the fair would close before they saw everything? Aunt Inas could talk to people any old time, but she and Jessie could see the fair only until it closed. So they had to hurry. Oh, yes, there was so much to see that they just had to keep moving.

And then it happened! Jessie spotted a large group of children over to one side of the exhibits. They were talking. In fact, it seemed that they all wanted to talk at once. What's so unusual about that? Well, nothing probably. But where do you suppose Jessie would rather be at a fair? With a lot of big people brushing horses and cows and talking, or with other children? Why, with other children, of course. Particularly when they were all talking so excitedly. Whom were they talking to anyway? Jessie decided that she and Aunt Inas would just have to go see. And that is exactly what they did. And you should have heard what Jessie and Aunt Inas heard. Yes, you really should have been there.

"Come on, Polly. Polly want a cracker?" one boy urged.

"Polly, Polly, want a cracker?" chimed in another.

"Aunt Inas, who is Polly? I don't see her anywhere. Who are they talking to anyway?" Jessie was bewildered. Polly just had to be someone important. But why were the children trying to make her eat crackers? Jessie wouldn't want just plain crackers either. Not at a fair.

"Pretty Polly, talk to us." A dark-haired girl was speaking, but apparently Polly wasn't talking to her, either. What a strange person! Why wouldn't she talk?

"Pretty Polly!"

"Polly want a cracker?"

"Talk to us, pretty Polly."

"Oh, she can't talk. She's just a dumb old bird!" exclaimed a boy in disgust.

A *bird!* Oh, Jessie just had to see that bird. Whoever heard of a bird talking anyway? She broke away from Aunt Inas and slipped between the children. And there it was. Yes, there it was. The largest bird Jessie had ever seen in her life. It was huge. And beautiful! That is, it surely had beautifully colored feathers. Its bill wasn't very beautiful, though. Jessie was utterly fascinated with that big bright bird!

"Polly want a cracker?"

"Come on, Polly. Say something."

"Cat got your tongue, Polly?"

The bird ignored her tormentors. She just sat there on her perch, preening herself and looking wise.

But there! What was that? Suddenly Polly came to life. Oh, yes, indeed! She stretched her neck and blinked her eyes. She peered down at the newcomer in that group. Yes, she stared right down at Jessie, and all of a sudden she talked. Yes, she did. In a funny harsh voice she shrieked, "Hello there, redhead! Hello there, redhead."

All those children just stood there with their mouths wide open, not saying a word. Then suddenly they began to laugh. They laughed and giggled and leaned against one another and laughed some more.

And Jessie? Well, Jessie didn't know whether to laugh or cry. After all, she was just a little girl. But she looked around at the children having such a merry time, and she laughed too. Then she looked up at that bright bird and said, "Why, hello there, Polly." Polly blinked one eye. Maybe she was winking. Maybe so, but Jessie never knew for sure.

TOM'S SONG

HEIGH-HO, HEIGH-HO, OLD cat sittin' on the hillside.'

" 'Heigh-ho, heigh-ho, old cat sittin' on the hillside.' "

Yes, it was working again! Sonny's eyelids were drooping lower and lower, and lower and lower, and presto! Sonny was asleep! How did Daddy do it? Jessie watched almost in disbelief. But she had to believe it, for Sonny certainly was asleep. And all Daddy had done was sing that simple little song over and over again. It really wasn't much of a tune, and you know the words already. Just "Heigh-ho, heigh-ho, old cat sittin' on the hillside." Maybe it was a magic song, because every time Daddy sang it, his voice getting slower and slower, Sonny went to sleep.

Daddy laughed when Jessie asked him if the song was magic. "I guess it must be," he replied. "It worked on Norine. Put her to sleep, just like that!"

"Did it really, Daddy? Just like with Sonny?" ·

"Of course, and it worked with you, too, and with Ilene and with Midget. All babies go to sleep when I sing that song."

Jessie wandered outside, still thinking about it. Just think! Sing a simple little song and babies go right to sleep! Well, *she* wasn't sleepy. No, indeed! In fact, she would really like to do something exciting. Like what? Well, she wasn't sure. She looked around. The sun was shining brightly. The sky was so blue, with bright clouds bumping and pushing one another around. But of course Jessie couldn't ride around on a cloud, even though that did sound like fun. But wait! She could ride in the hammock. That was it! Just the thing! Now, it so happened that Norine was in the hammock, reading a book. Norine was always reading a book, and that really wasn't much fun. Well, even though Norine seemed to be enjoying the hammock, Jessie decided that was the very thing that she wanted to do. But what about Norine? Oh, well, she had had the hammock long enough.

"I want to swing in the hammock, Norine," said Jessie firmly.

"But I'm here first, and I'm reading," protested Norine.

"I want this hammock now. You can read your old book on the porch. I want to swing."

"No, I was here first. After a while it will be your turn. Go away!"

Now, don't you think that Norine was right? Jessie probably thought so too, but she did want that hammock right at that very moment.

"I'll swing with you." Jessie plopped down by her unwilling sister, and digging her toes into the sand underneath, sent the hammock swinging.

"Stop, Jessie. I can't read with you sitting almost on top of me and making the hammock bump all over the place. If you want to be in with me, sit still, and I'll read you a story."

Sit still and read a story? On a day like this, with that blue sky and those bumping, pushing clouds? No way! "No, Norine. I want to swing as high as the sky!" And kicking her feet, Jessie again sent the hammock sailing.

Norine held on tightly for a few minutes, and then, tears sliding down her cheeks, she climbed out of the hammock and started for the house.

Jessie seemed not to mind at all. Merrily she sang, " 'Heigh-ho, heigh-ho, old cat sittin' on the hillside. Heigh-ho . . .' " She laughed at the clouds skudding across the sky. There! That one was a big white cat, its long tail swishing. And that one was a little lamb jumping over a cloud of daisies. And there was an old man with long white whiskers flowing way down over his chest. It looked something like Uncle Dow! Oh, the world was beautiful, and Jessie's voice rose and shrieked, " 'Heigh-ho, heigh-ho!' "

Norine reached the house and raised her tear-stained face to Mommy. Mommy didn't say a word, but lifted her onto a chair and pointed outside toward the Slater place across the street. Together they watched.

" 'Heigh-ho, heigh-ho, old cat sittin' on the hillside.' " Hm-m-m!

Now, a very fierce pet lived at the Slaters'. Pet? Well, maybe he wasn't exactly a pet. He was a great big, tough old tom turkey. You had just better believe that no children wandered into the Slaters' back yard without that turkey's seeing them. And if old Tom Turkey saw them, well, no one, not even the nice little Williams children, dared walk past him. And if Victor Slater wanted to play with any neighborhood children, he went to *their* place.

Now old Tom Turkey cocked his head and listened. What is that unearthly noise? he probably thought to himself, if turkeys think like that. Maybe it sounded like a turkey love call. A love call sounding like that? Oh, it couldn't be. It must be a battle cry. Whatever it was, Tom meant to put a stop to it. *Gobble, gobble, gobble,* he answered. The noise across the street continued.

" 'Heigh-ho, heigh-ho.' "

And the answer returned, *Gobble, gobble, gobble.*

Jessie kicked harder, and the hammock squeaked between the two big maple trees. Jessie's song grew wilder and louder. Old Tom became a little bit angry. It's a sure thing that *he* wasn't gradually falling asleep as Sonny did when Daddy sang. But the singer wasn't Daddy, and the listener wasn't Sonny. No, sir! Old Tom's tail feathers began to spread out into a beautiful fan, the pride of his turkey heart, and in a voice that should have warned anyone that he meant business, he sang out his own war cry—*Gobble, gobble, gobble!*

Still that loud warble came from beneath the maple trees across the way. " 'Heigh-ho, heigh-ho, old cat sittin' on the hillside.' "

Now, Tom Turkey knew his place. Yes, he did. Maybe he wouldn't let any children into his yard, but that didn't mean that he trespassed on anyone else's property. Of course not. He stayed in his own back yard, tending to his own business. Never was he found guilty of going one step beyond the gate. But what was a turkey to do? Old Tom was very angry by this time. He absolutely would not tolerate any kind of rival. And he wasn't going to stand for that loud song from beneath the maple trees. He would stop it once and for all. Long neck stretched high, fantail spread to its limit, fire in his eye, he marched across the street to do battle with that insulting bird, whoever it might be.

Of course, Jessie didn't know what was happening. If she had known that old Tom Turkey was headed her way, do you think she

would have stayed a single minute? Oh, no. Not she. And you wouldn't have stayed either. Not if you had known old Tom Turkey as all the neighborhood children knew him. But Jessie didn't know that Tom was coming, so on and on she sang.

It didn't take that turkey long to cross the street and march into the Williams yard. It didn't take him long to reach the hammock between the two tall maple trees. And it didn't take him long to do what he did next. And what was that? No one really knows for sure, for it happened so fast that even Mommy and Norine, watching from the house, couldn't tell. Did he lift one sharp-toed foot and push that hammock upside down, or did he do it with his head and strong neck? Jessie should be able to tell you, but she couldn't either. All she knew was that suddenly she got a terrific bump from behind, and out of the hammock she flew and right smack down into all that soft sandy dust beneath.

The worst of it was that she landed on her face. Poor Jessie! Oh, no, she didn't really get hurt, but just think of being boosted out of a hammock by an old turkey gobbler! Jessie was ready to run for her life, but she soon knew there was no need to run. None whatsoever. Old Tom Turkey had done what he came to do and was headed for home, head high, tail feathers still spread. No need for him to hang around in someone else's yard. Jessie gave him one quick look, then, tears spilling down her cheeks, she opened her mouth to howl! But just then she glanced up and saw Mommy and Norine at the window. Jessie hardly knew what to think. It seemed as if they were ready to burst out laughing.

Jessie suddenly saw a very unlovely picture. No, it wasn't a picture of old Tom Turkey pushing her out of the hammock. No, nothing like that. She saw a picture of a red-haired little girl pushing her *own sister* out of the hammock. She knew that probably turkeys had a right to push noisy little girls out of a hammock. Yes, she supposed that was a turkey's right. And she knew that she had been pretty mean to Norine, and Norine hadn't done one thing to her.

No, Jessie didn't cry. She just hung her head. And Mommy did just the thing that your own mother would do for you. She just reached out and put her arm around her naughty little girl and hugged her. And Norine did just what a nice sweet sister would do. She reached out and began to brush the dust out of Jessie's hair and off her clothes. And

Jessie did what any little girl would do when she saw how naughty she had been and how kind everyone was to her. She just reached one arm around Mommy. And she reached the other arm around Norine, and said, "Mommy, Norine, I'm sorry that I was so mean. I guess you won't need to spank me this time. Slaters' old tom turkey spanked me. I think I'll remember that spanking all my life." And I'm sure she did remember.

MOVE IT, SONNY!

SNIFF! SNIFF! "UM-M-M!"
What was that strange odor? Strange, but so fresh and clean and delightful? Could it be——? Yes, it really was! The cedar shakes had that lovely, sweet, clean, fresh smell. And those clean, fresh cedar shakes were everywhere. In fact, the whole woodshed was built with cedar shakes. Daddy had split them himself. And with them he had also built a sidewalk from the back door of the Williams house to Aunt Molly's place. He had built another sidewalk to the woodshed, and a cedar sidewalk led to the pump and to the root house, which was built of cedar also.

No, this wasn't in Burlington. This wasn't a high house with a cool dirt basement under it. This new home was a bunkhouse in a logging camp called Camp Six. Oh, maybe you don't know a thing about logging camps and bunkhouses and speeders and handcars and donkeys and such, so I'd better tell you a few things. In the logging camps a long time ago there were bunkhouses grouped around the kitchen and dining room. The loggers, men who cut down trees and loaded them onto trains, lived in the bunkhouses and ate their meals all together in the cookhouse. Well, this particular logging camp had special bunkhouses divided into rooms for families to live in. And that is where the Williams family lived. Maybe you think that wasn't fun! Well, the Williams children loved their new home.

Each girl had a playhouse of her own. Where? Why, right up on top of the big stumps that were everywhere around their bunkhouse home. Oh, those stumps were huge. Four feet, six feet, eight feet, and sometimes ten or twelve feet across. Daddy cut notches in the bark for steps so the children could walk right up to the flat tops, where they had their playhouse. Of course, the playhouses didn't have any roofs on them, but still they were lots of fun.

Then there was the canyon right back of the house. This canyon ran behind all the family houses in the camp, and it was an extraspecial place to play. The sides of the canyon were lined with lush ferns and grasses and logs, just the best place in the world for a game of hide-and-seek. And way down at the bottom of the canyon, trickling this way and that, flowed a little half-hidden creek. Now, you know all about little creeks and water wheels and little boats that go sailing, and boys and girls wading in the hot summertime.

And the donkey! Oh, I suppose you have seen a donkey, all right. A donkey with big long ears and all that, but I don't mean *that* kind. This donkey was used to drag logs in from the woods, but it wasn't an animal. It was a big piece of machinery. It had two large spools, bigger even than the fourth-grade boys. On these spools were rolled yards and yards of cable. Everything about the donkey smelled of oil. And oil smells almost as good as cedar wood, only different.

Then there were the trestles, railroad bridges across the canyons. A boy or girl could fall through these bridges if he or she didn't have hold of Daddy's hand. Because, you see, they were built with large logs or pilings reaching up from below. On these from one end of the canyon to the other were strung more logs. Then ties, or long squared pieces of wood, were put across. On top of these were placed the rails, and that was a railroad bridge, or trestle. If you walked across on the ties, and if you had your eyes open as you really should, and if you looked down, you could see through the open spaces clear to the bottom of the canyon. Oh, that could be very scary. Then you would probably quit looking down right then because you would probably be getting pretty dizzy. The best way was to watch the ties just ahead of your feet as you walked; then you could go across easily.

There were many children living in that logging camp. Of course, when the big ones were away at school, the smaller ones didn't have quite so much fun. It would have been lonesome for Midget and Sonny, with Norine, Jessie, and Ilene gone to school, if it hadn't been for that woodshed with the good cedar smell all around. Midget and Sonny were too little to go down into the canyon; they were too little to get up on the stump playhouses; the big donkey was too far away for them to go to all alone; and, of course, they wouldn't even think of walking on the trestles! No, never! But they could play in the woodshed, and it really was the very nicest place of all to play.

That is, it *should* have been the very nicest place of all to play, and it would have been IF—— Midget thought it was because of Sonny, and Sonny thought it was because of Midget!

"You can't have the door there!" burst out Sonny crossly. Oh, Sonny wasn't a baby any longer. In fact, he was 3 years old and Midget was a year and a half older. Sonny was old enough to have a few ideas about things, and he was sure he knew what he wanted and he knew he was right. Sonny was very displeased with Midget.

"You can't have a door here. I won't let you!" Sonny put one chubby little hand on the chopping block. "Our door isn't going to be here. It has to be over there!" And he pointed to one end of the woodpile.

Midget placed both hands on her hips. Her black eyes flashed as she looked at her brother. Sonny was certainly stubborn. He just wouldn't listen to her anymore. Whatever was the matter with him?

"Sonny Williams"—Midget stamped her foot angrily—"you listen to me!" Suddenly she turned and grabbed the ax from its place in the corner. "You move that hand, Sonny Williams, or I'll cut it right off!"

Midget was shocked at herself! No one was allowed to even touch the axes! If you did touch one you would get an awful spanking, a really hard one. Now, you know that nobody wants to be spanked at all, but a really hard spanking—oh, NO!

Midget had dared to pick up the ax! What would happen now? Daddy had never spanked any of the four girls, and he had never spanked Sonny, either. But he had meant it when he had said to never, never, *never* touch the axes! Now Midget would be spanked. Hard! Sonny decided he wouldn't tell on her. He wouldn't make her be spanked, even though she really should be. Besides, Sonny knew she was just fooling. She would never cut off his hand. Of course not!

"I won't move my hand. The door is going to be over there and no place else," Sonny said loudly.

"Oh, you bad boy! Move your hand or I'll cut it right off!" Midget was very angry.

"I won't!"

"Yes, you will!"

"I won't, either."

"You'd better or I'll cut it off right there." And Midget traced a line right across Sonny's fat little wrist.

"No, sir! We can't have the door here. You don't dare cut my hand off! You'll get spanked for having that ax, too." And Sonny kept his hand right there on the chopping block.

"Move it!"

"I won't!"

Midget was so angry that tears were beginning to fill her eyes. And when you get that angry, things begin to get bad.

"Sonny, for the last time, move your hand. Now!"

Sonny was very, very angry too. He was sure Midget was just bluffing. He wasn't moving his hand just to please her! No way!

"We aren't going to have the door here, and I'm not going to move my hand. You put that ax over in the corner where it belongs, right now!"

Now something very bad was growing in Midget's heart. All of a sudden she wasn't thinking like a nice, sweet little girl who loved her brother dearly. The ax was pretty heavy for her, but with both arms she raised it above her head and brought it down! Thud! It hit something and then toppled out of her grasp. But, look! Sonny hadn't moved his hand. Oh, she had been sure he would move it. Why hadn't he? Blood was pouring out of Sonny's hand. Midget just looked at him helplessly; then all of a sudden tears poured down her cheeks. With a huge, squalling cry she turned and plunged toward the house.

"Mommy, Mommy! Come here! Hurry! Sonny's hand is cut off!" She grabbed Mommy's skirt and tugged for her to come. Well, Mommy didn't need to be told that something was wrong. Not with that awful screaming from Midget and that other horrible shrieking coming from the woodshed! Mommy practically flew out there, stumbling over Midget, who managed to get right in the way. And here came Aunt Molly. And here came Mrs. Holeman and Mrs. Murphy; and Merritt and Merton, the little twin neighbor boys; and their mother. Everywhere in camp screen doors slammed and people came running over to the Williamses' woodshed!

Aunt Molly was just like a nurse, and she didn't lose her head like some of the ladies were doing. She grabbed Sonny's hand and put the dangling part back up tight against the whole part. Then she wrapped some clean cloths around it. Then she grabbed a shingle, placed Sonny's hand on it, wrapped shingle and hand all up together, and sent for Daddy to come from the camp. It wasn't long until he came. There were only one or two automobiles in the camp at that time so long ago, but someone came with a car, and away went Sonny and Daddy to the doctor's place many miles away.

That was a pretty exciting ride, because the driver made that car go as fast as it could over the bumpy road. The doctor was very kind and kept saying that everything was going to be all right. It wasn't long until he had made a neat row of stitches across the hurt hand. Sonny became pretty proud of his stitches and of the big scar that grew where the cut had been. But he was ashamed, and so was Midget, when they thought of how they had let Satan make them so unkind to each other. No, they didn't get a spanking, not even a gentle one. They had learned their lesson. Never again were they tempted to even put a hand on the ax that stood in the corner. Never again!

"DAD" THOMPSON

MOMMY SLUMPED DEjectedly on a wooden crate. Big boxes, little boxes, cartons and crates, crocks and buckets, were all piled in confusion on the kitchen floor. Huge iron bed frames and springs were flopped against the wall. A kerosene lamp flickered over the messy room and was reflected in each bare, night-shadowed windowpane.

"Mommy, I'm hungry," moaned Ilene as she huddled dismally against a mattress.

"Mommy, I'm all shivery," sobbed Midget from the shadows.

Norine rocked Baby James, trying to soothe his unhappiness or hunger pains or whatever it was that was bothering him. Little Sonny just stared at Daddy and didn't say a word. Neither did Jessie, although she felt like saying something real mean. She was hungry and tired and cold and just miserable!

You are probably wondering why everyone was in such an unhappy mood. Well, it's a little hard to explain unless you have had to move from a nice, comfortable bunkhouse at Camp Six to a big empty house in Laurel Heights. Sometimes moving isn't all that bad, but it can be terrible when the day turns out to be rainy and the horse and wagon and driver don't get to your Camp Six house to load until after noon and you and all the older children have to walk to the new home in the rain! You are cold and wet before you ever get there, and, of course, while you are waiting for Mommy and Daddy and Sonny and Baby James to come on the wagon, a wheel or something breaks and you just have to wait and wait and wait!

"Jessie, you look just like a storm cloud," Mommy exclaimed, half laughing and half irritated. Of course, Mommy was just as cold and wet and hungry and miserable as any of them, but somehow Jessie didn't seem to remember that.

"I hate this new house! Why couldn't we have stayed at Camp Six? I wish Daddy would hurry and get the stovepipe fixed so that we could have some supper!" Oh, how cross Jessie was, and what a temper she was showing.

"Now, Jessie, just be patient. You aren't suffering a bit more than the other children. Look how Norine is acting. She's even trying to keep the baby happy," Mommy soothed.

Well, Jessie knew that Mommy was right, but do you know something? It made Jessie even more furious to be told how nicely Norine was behaving! Oh, that girl!

Jessie and the other children and Mommy were not the only ones having problems. You should have seen Daddy. Of course, you may not know too much about how people always had to put up stovepipes in the olden days. The cookstove had to have a stovepipe to carry the smoke out through the upstairs and through the roof and away. You couldn't cook a meal until that stovepipe was up. And sometimes it could be very stubborn. And that is exactly the way it was that cold, miserable, wet evening! Daddy would just get that pipe to fit into the stove and it would pop out up at the elbow where it went into the wall. Then when he would finally get the elbow fixed, out would pop the end that fitted into the stove.

Some people might have grown so exasperated that they would have just taken that stovepipe and heaved it right out the door. That would have been a pretty silly thing to do, of course, and Daddy just wasn't that kind of silly person. No, he was so very patient and good. He knew how his little family were suffering. He wanted to get that stove and stovepipe set up and a nice warm fire burning. He knew as well as anyone that people can be much more cheerful and happy when they are warm and have something to eat. Yes, he knew all that, and he was trying his very best to get that stovepipe fixed, but it was "a real bear." That's what he called it, a real bear!

As the whole family huddled in gloomy misery, there came a soft knock at the door. Now, the strange thing about that quiet knock was that no one had heard a single footstep. A knock, but no sound of feet on the steps or on the porch? That can send some funny-feeling shivers right up your back, can't it?

"Mommy, what's that?" Ilene's eyes had grown large with fright. Sonny quit watching Daddy and backed up close to Mommy and stared at the door. No one said a word, and everyone drew closer together. What else could happen on this awful night?

The knock came again. All thoughts of hunger and cold vanished quick as a flash! Everyone was very still. No one moved. Even Baby James hushed his fussing.

"Will someone please answer the door?" Daddy asked from his perch on top of the cookstove.

The knock sounded the third time. Mommy slowly stepped to the door and very cautiously drew it open. On the threshold stood a thin, hunchbacked man. He was old, with straggly hair showing beneath a blue denim hat. He was dressed in blue denim coveralls and a blue denim coat. He stepped quickly inside, and with a friendly grin on his wrinkled face he held out a bucket, a beautiful old tin bucket, full of foamy white milk. He seemed not to notice all the frightened eyes staring at him. Mommy looked rather scared too, but she accepted the offering just the same. Then from one large denim pocket he pulled a loaf of bread. From the other denim pocket he drew out another package, which, with a quick flip, he tossed into Ilene's lap. Ilene gasped, and all the Williams children gathered closer to see what the stranger had given her.

"Oh, it's pink peppermints!" squealed Jessie.

"Pink peppermints!" Sonny burbled. "Let me see."

Everyone wanted to see and to feel and to touch. Pink peppermints! How wonderful! With no more introduction than that the Williams children accepted their new neighbor in blue denim as their friend forever.

"How are you coming with that stove, neighbor?" he asked Daddy.

"Well, now that you ask, I must say that I'm not getting far, that's sure." And Daddy rubbed a sooty arm across his already sooty face.

"Well, you are probably needing a good pair of hands to help you a bit. Here, let's see what I can do." And the new friend climbed up on the stove beside Daddy and went to work. Almost as quick as a wink that stovepipe fell right into place, Daddy built a fire, and soon he and the blue-denim man were busy setting up beds. The new friend told the Williams family that his name was Thompson; Daddy right then began calling him "Dad," and he became Dad Thompson to the whole neighborhood.

Norine and Jessie and Ilene and Midget and Sonny soon became well acquainted with old Dad Thompson. Why? Well, yes, he always had some pink peppermints tucked in a pocket. But that wasn't the only reason. You see, he was the janitor at the school. Oh, not just an ordinary janitor. Oh, no! At his magic touch the fires glowed brightly. The water bucket glistened with clean, sparkling water. The floors were always swept and shining, because that's the way he wanted it. Even the teachers' faces beamed at his gentle jokes. The school and all that belonged to it was his in a special way.

Even the schoolchildren were his in a special way too. Do you know why? Well, because he built their monkey bars at school. He planned all the games at the school picnics. Yes, that's right. All the potato races and the sack races and the three-legged races and the little kids' races, and the big kids' races and even the old ladies' races. He taught all the little first- and second-graders how to hold the smoothed-off board to bat the ball correctly. And he played horseshoes with all the daddies. Any birthday or holiday was an occasion to celebrate. He pampered the children and scolded them sometimes, too, when they really needed it. He could even fix dolls and swings. Yes, he could.

After a few days Jessie forgot that she had ever said she hated the new house or that she wished her family still lived at Camp Six. Oh, yes, she forgot all about such things. This new place was the nicest place in all the world to live. Why? Well, you would have thought so too if you lived right next door to the most wonderful person in the world, old Dad Thompson, the wonderful pink-peppermint friend.

ALWAYS
A LITTLE
BOY

WHEN ORR WAS BORN HE was just like all other babies—at least that is what old Dad Thompson said. He grew, began to laugh and gurgle, and soon was crawling around and climbing up beside a chair. And suddenly he was walking. Now, that seems to be pretty much the way babies grow, doesn't it?

By and by, when Orr was about 2 years old, he began to say words, and soon he was talking. Everything was going fine, but suddenly Orr seemed different. His body kept on growing, but the way he thought and talked and understood was like a very little boy. He could play games just like other children if they were simple games. He liked to play with toys if they were simple toys. He liked to run and jump just like any young boy. But Orr just kept on doing things like a little boy, even when he grew taller than his dad. No matter how many birthdays passed, inside himself Orr was always just a little boy. This was very hard on Dad Thompson, because, you see, Orr didn't have a mother. She had died when he was very small. Dad Thompson had to cook Orr's meals and wash and iron his clothes and make his bed and take care of him just as if he were a very young child, even though he was a big grown man.

One morning not long after the Williams family moved into their new Laurel Heights home, Orr came to visit. Oh, he probably heard the girls and Sonny and James shouting as they played and explored their new home. Yes, he probably heard them, and suddenly he wanted to go to their place and play, too. So he came running through the field and up the hill to the Williams house.

Suddenly the children's laughter hushed, and they stood there staring at Orr. Who was that big, tall young man? Whoever he was, the

Williams children decided that he must be a friend because he stood there looking happy, with a wide, friendlygrin overspreading his face.

"I want to play with you," he said simply.

"Play with us?" they gasped. A big man wanting to play with them? Why, whoever had heard of such a thing?

"Yes. Let me play too."

Mom, noting the sudden silence outdoors, came to the porch to look the situation over. Mothers do that every once in a while, particularly if things become too quiet, you know. When she saw the tall young man with the children she said, "Oh, good morning, Orr. Did you come to play?"

Orr glanced up. His smile grew even wider and happier when he saw Mom. She was a very pretty woman with blue, blue eyes and dark-brown hair, you will remember. Not only that, her kind ways made her even more beautiful. She stood there on the porch, smiling pleasantly. Orr just looked at Mom. He realized that in some way she belonged to these children. He accepted her as someone nice and good and kind. Someone in authority. Someone to be obeyed. Someone like his dad.

"I came to play," Orr said. This sounded very strange to the children, but Mom knew all about Orr already. She told the children to go ahead with their games and let him play too. She nodded at them reassuringly. Even though the children didn't quite understand, they trusted their mother and continued with their games. They laughed and laughed when they were playing follow-the-leader and they came to the bars across the road. Orr didn't crawl through the bars as they did. He just swung one leg over and then the other. When they, one by one, climbed a small tree and swung from its top, Orr just stood grinning at them. He couldn't do that because he was almost as large as the tree.

Orr got in the habit of going with the Williams children to the house for lunch. Mom never thought of sending him home. No, indeed. She would just butter a slice of bread for him, too. Orr liked the children. He liked their games. He liked eating sandwiches and fruit with the family. But best of all he liked Mom. Yes, Orr just adored her. The poor fellow didn't have a mother of his own, you know. Just think how terrible that would be!

One day Orr went up to play with the children as usual. Then he joined them for a sandwich and fruit. Now, it was almost time for the Fourth of July picnic, and you already know how much fun that can be! Mom had wooden boxes scattered around the kitchen. Back in those days people didn't have cardboard cartons. And Mom didn't seem to be too fond of those heavy wooden boxes, for this is what she said: "I wish I had a picnic basket for our lunch! When I have to pack enough lunch for all you children in these heavy wooden boxes, one can hardly lift the things. Yes, I wish I had a picnic basket!"

"What's a picnic basket? Isn't it heavy, too?" asked Sonny.

"Oh, no, not like these wooden boxes," sighed Mom. "A picnic basket is made out of light reeds woven together. It has handles so that you can carry it easily, and there is a cover on top. You can pack lots of food in one and it still is not too heavy. With a family this size, we need something like that."

Now, Orr knew what a basket was. He gathered eggs from the henhouse in a basket. Yes, he knew about baskets, and he became troubled. Mrs. Williams wanted a big basket. He knew his little egg basket wasn't what she wanted. Orr went home, but through his child's mind ran the words about the picnic basket. Mom wanted a basket, a big basket to carry lots of lunch in. Orr felt that nothing would please him more than to find a basket for Mrs. Williams. But where? He didn't know.

Not long after Orr had heard Mom's spoken desire for a basket, he and his dad went down the lane, crossed the bars at the gate, and went past the Danker place, on past the school, over the hill where the church stood, then down the other side to the store. As Orr wandered around the store while his dad bought a new milk pail and some other items, he suddenly spied something. Mom would like that, he thought. He kept looking around the store, but his eyes always drifted back to the perfect gift for Mom.

Soon Dad Thompson called Orr to come, and the two of them trudged up and over the hill toward home. Orr didn't say much to his dad, but he kept on thinking and thinking and thinking. The next day he didn't stop to play with the Williams children. No, he just walked on by, through the meadow, and all the way to the store. He stepped inside and before very long came out carrying the perfect gift, the gift for the beautiful mom who fixed sandwiches for him and the other children.

As Orr walked along, his smile grew wide. He was going to make Mom happy. He would give her a gift. It seemed like no time at all until he was at the Williamses' back door.

"Mrs. Williams," he called, then more loudly, "Mom!" After all, Mom was what all the children called her.

Mom heard Orr and called, "Come on in, Orr. We are having lunch. Would you like a sandwich?"

Orr stepped into the kitchen. Mom looked at him, and her eyes widened in surprise. "Whatever do you have there?" she asked.

"It's for you, Mrs. Williams. It's a picnic basket." Orr's face beamed as he offered his gift of love.

It was a basket, all right, but it wasn't exactly what Mom had in mind. It had no lid. It had no handles that crossed over the top. It was a very large, very ordinary clothes basket with handles on each side. Small handles. It had slanted sides, too, not a bit like a picnic basket.

"It will carry lots of picnic lunch, Mrs. Williams," Orr said happily.

"Why, that is just what I wanted. A lovely picnic basket!" Mom exclaimed as she smiled at Orr, who just beamed. All the children gathered round to admire the basket that Orr had brought.

Orr soon left, his mission accomplished. And he was happy.

Mom, however, was puzzled. And she was worried. Where had Orr gotten the clothes basket? Where had he gotten the money to pay for it? When Dad came home she told him all about it.

"Where do you suppose he got it, Jim?" she asked. "And where did he get the money. You know Dad Thompson wouldn't give him any cash. The poor child wouldn't know how to handle it."

"Did the basket have any wrappings on it?" asked Dad. "Perhaps if it had we would have some idea where it came from."

"No, there were no wrappings," said Mom. "He just came in carrying it in his hands. No tags, no wrappings, nothing at all."

"Just don't worry anymore." Mr. Williams smiled at his wife. "I'll see what I can find out about it. I don't think you should say anything to Dad Thompson yet. Maybe we can solve this without hurting either of them."

Dad picked up his hat, opened the door, then paused for a moment. "Now, remember, mum's the word. That means you children, too." He closed the door and was gone.

"Mr. Gibson," Dad asked when he entered the store, "do you have any large wicker clothes baskets with sloping sides and small handles on each end?"

Mr. Gibson thought a moment, then replied, "Well, we did have four or five of them, but they are probably all sold. Wait a minute." He paused in thought, then continued, "I remember seeing one left in the back of the store. Come on, we'll check it out and see if it is what you are looking for."

Mr. Gibson led the way to the rear of the store and looked around. There was no basket such as Dad had described. "No, sir, I guess we must have sold it. I know it was here a couple of days ago." Then a thought occurred to him. "Just a second more, Mr. Williams. I'll ask my wife. Perhaps she has moved it.

"Madge, did you sell that large clothes basket we had in back?" he called to Mrs. Gibson, who was stacking some bolts of cloth in the dry-goods department.

Mrs. Gibson turned, greeted Mr. Williams, and said, "No, Joe. I didn't sell it. It must be here somewhere." She joined the two men at the back of the store.

"H'mmm!" Mr. Gibson puzzled aloud. "What could have happened to that basket? I don't recall having sold it."

Then Mr. Williams explained to the two about Mom's new picnic basket. He told them how Mom had remarked how much she would like to have one and how Orr had come carrying home a clothes basket that he thought was a picnic basket.

Now, Orr could have been in bad trouble. He had stolen a valuable clothes basket, hadn't he? He hadn't paid one penny for it, had he? He had given it to Mom because she was such a good, sweet mother to her own children and to him, also. Orr, who had no mother.

"I'll tell you what I'll do," said Mr. Williams. "I'll pay for the basket. Mom needs one anyway. Please don't say anything to Dad Thompson," he added. "No use bothering him."

Mr. and Mrs. Gibson agreed to say nothing. The basket was paid for and all was well.

"Perhaps you should watch Orr just in case he gets into the habit of taking things. We don't want that to happen," suggested Mr. Williams. The Gibsons agreed.

When Mr. Williams arrived home he told Mrs. Williams and the older children all about the basket and how he had paid the price for it. "Let's bury this secret of Orr and the picnic basket deep down, way out of sight, shall we?" Dad suggested.

Mom and the children readily agreed. After all, they liked Orr and didn't want him to get into any trouble. And the basket was paid for and truly belonged to them now.

And do you know, Orr never stole another single thing from the store. Dad Thompson never knew and neither did any of the neighbors.

Do you know that we are all like Orr? Oh, yes, we are. We do things that are wrong. Then Jesus, who knows our heart, says, "I've paid for the mistake that child made. Let's forgive him (her)." Our heavenly Father agrees, so the debt is paid. But not by us. And because Jesus paid for our sins with His life, we can be free. We are no longer guilty. Just like Orr was free. Isn't God wonderful! Isn't Jesus wonderful!

I DARE YOU!

ONE OF THE VERY NICEST things on the earth is a best friend. Yes, that's right. Best friends hardly ever get angry at you. They always want to come to your place to play or they want you to go to their place to play. Either way is perfectly all right when you are best friends. Now, if your best friend just happens to be someone like Mabel, then you know what a best friend really is!

Jessie and Mabel became best friends when both lived at Camp Six. Jessie, as you know, had reddish hair and hazel eyes. Mabel had dark-brown hair and green eyes. So you see, they didn't look much alike. Jessie was a few months older than Mabel, and so started to school sooner, but Mabel could do ever so many things much better than Jessie. She could run faster. She could build paddle wheels for playing in the creek at Camp Six. She could build birdhouses. She could do forward skin the cat on the monkey bars long before Jessie could. She could stand on her head and she could turn cartwheels. Mom called Mabel a tomboy. Tomboy or not, Jessie wished she could be just like her. Maybe that was what caused all the weeping and trouble that awful day. Yes, maybe it was all Mabel's fault, but then again, maybe it was all Jessie's fault. She was older, you know.

The trouble began on the day of the school picnic. What? Trouble at a picnic? That's silly! You don't have trouble at a picnic. You play lots of games and eat and eat until you just can't eat anymore. And you chase one another and go wading until you are so tired that you are glad when Mom calls that it is time to go home. Yes, that is the way picnics are. But hold on a minute! Maybe you should say that that is the way picnics are *supposed* to be. That is the way picnics usually are. But sometimes they just aren't that way at all. And that's too bad!

This special picnic should have been just grand. The reason? Why, because old Dad Thompson, the pink-peppermint friend, was in charge of the games. And it started out fun. Really, it did. It started out with the girls' footrace, which Mabel won easily. Then there was the peanut race. Midget won that. Mabel won the potato race. She won the sack race, too. Jessie was sure Mabel won the sack race because she managed to bump into anyone who came close to her. As a result that unlucky person went sprawling while Mabel bounced merrily on.

Then it came time for the three-legged race, and Mabel and Jessie were partners. That's the way with best friends, you know.

"We're going to win this race, Mabel," Jessie remarked to her friend, with a grin.

"Yeah, I know," responded Mabel, with a happy tug at the binder around their legs.

Jessie's spirits soared as she kept her eyes riveted on old Dad Thompson and the big red bandanna handkerchief held high in his hand. She was teamed up with the winner of the day, so this victory would be hers as well as Mabel's.

"Get ready!" Dad Thompson paused, enjoying the excitement of each couple before him.

"Get set!" Knees trembled! Hearts thumped!

"Go!" And down came the red bandanna and away joggled all the couples. Then the fun began. Here and there a pair would stumble and fall laughing to the ground. Another couple would grow nervous, and over into a heap they would tumble. Jessie and Mabel struggled along for three or four steps, then down they went. But it was early in the race, and both were confident they could still win. They untangled their mixed-up legs. All the while they were getting to their feet, Mabel was explaining to Jessie that they had to put their outside legs forward at the same time, then their inside legs forward together at the same time.

On they went, rather grimly now. Suddenly something happened again. Somehow one of Jessie's legs got ahead of one of Mabel's and down they went a second time.

"I told you to put your leg forward right at the same time I do," Mabel sputtered.

"That's just what I did. Besides, who made you my boss?" Jessie was furious. Her face was as red as her hair.

"Well, come on! We can still win the race if we hurry. There are lots of others down," urged Mabel.

Jessie sulkily agreed, and up and away they started. But it didn't go well. Before long there were Jessie and Mabel all tangled on the ground. This time their binder had broken. The race was all over for them.

"You clumsy old cow!" Mabel threw the strap angrily. "I'll never let you be my partner again!"

"Who wants to be your partner, anyway? You can't even run a three-legged race! I wouldn't let you be my partner again if you paid me a hundred dollars!" scolded Jessie, and away she stalked.

And that's the way the day began. When it came lunchtime Jessie sat with one group of girls and Mabel sat with another. Two little best friends were very unhappy.

Then came the afternoon of the picnic. The best friends were still angry, even after the ice cream. No, the afternoon part of the picnic wasn't going to be any better than the morning had. And that was too bad. The mothers of all the little girls had agreed that the girls could play in the water down by the old bridge across the Pilchuck River. The Pilchuck wasn't a big river. It wasn't a wide river. In fact, some people called it the Pilchuck Creek. Yes, the girls could play down by the bridge, but no one, absolutely no one, was to go across the gravel bar to the deep side. But they all knew that already. That was where the men and older boys sometimes went swimming. Well, who wanted to play over there anyway? There were deep holes over there where a person could go underwater and drown, so, of course, all the children promised to play on the shallow side of the gravel bar.

Jessie ducked down into the shallow water and splashed her hands and feet wildly. She was pretending that she was swimming. Then came Mabel's teasing voice.

"Pooh, you think that's swimming? You're a fraidycat. Little old second-grader thinks she's big. Ha-ha!"

Fraidycat, was she? Jessie's face grew red and her eyes shot sparks. Who did Mabel think she was? She wasn't so smart! She was just a big noise, that was all. Well, Jessie was just not going to pay a speck of attention to Mabel. That would show her!

Mabel had watched Jessie lying in the water splashing her arms and legs. It did look like fun and it did look almost like swimming. Now she decided to try it.

"Ho-ho! Mud-crawlin' turtle, that's all you are," jeered Jessie as she watched.

"Well, how about you? You're a bullfrog!" Mabel's voice was shrill.

"And you're a long-snout mud hog," taunted Jessie. Oh, such naughty girls and such terrible things they were saying to each other! "I'll bet you don't dare swim over to the deep water!" Jessie dared.

Mabel was shocked. Go over to the deep water? Go where they were forbidden ever to go? Why, she certainly didn't want to go over there. No, sir! No way!

Yes, that is what Mabel thought, but that isn't what she said. No, indeed! She said, "Huh! I'll bet YOU don't dare swim through the deep water and then come back!"

Jessie wavered a little, then replied, "I'll bet I do dare. Huh! I'm not scared of the deep water!"

"All right, then, let's see you go across!"

"Well, if you want to go so bad, why don't you just strike out and go? You're the one who's afraid, that's why!" goaded Jessie.

Mabel thought about the deep holes over on the other side. Holes that you might step into and in which you could disappear from sight and drown. She also knew that to go there would be disobeying.

"See, I told you so. You're afraid." Jessie's voice was taunting.

What should Mabel do? "Huh! You just think I'm afraid, don't you? Well, just watch me!" And away Mabel flounced, though not very fast. She reached the gravel bar, then paused. "I can go across the deep water easy, but I'll bet you don't dare, Jessie."

"I can do anything you can do, Mabel. So there!" Quickly Jessie joined Mabel on the gravel bar.

"Jessie, you come back here! Don't you dare go into that deep water. Remember what Mom said!" called Norine from the safety of the shallow water.

Yes, Jessie remembered. And she was scared. How she wanted to go back. How she wished Mabel would suggest it.

But Mabel stepped into the water. It was over her knees. Frightened, she looked at Jessie, who stared back at her, then stepped into the water right beside her. Mabel stepped forward another step. Wow! The water certainly got deep awfully fast on this side of the gravel bar. Its wet coldness was lapping around her hips. Well, Mabel determined to go another step just to prove her courage to Jessie. But again Jessie stepped right up beside her.

"I'll bet you're afraid to go first, Jessie. I just bet you're afraid."

Jessie looked down at the dark-brown water. She looked ahead and couldn't see a thing. Perhaps she would take just one more teensy, tiny little step. She did, and the water was suddenly above her waist, almost to her shoulders. The girls back in the shallow area were screaming and crying. Oh, thought Jessie, this is awful, just awful! Why doesn't Mabel go back?

But, no, Mabel stepped right up beside her. "Does this deep, deep water give you cold feet, mud turtle?" she taunted. The girls glared at each other.

"No, it doesn't. You're the one who's scared. Why don't you just admit you're scared, Mabel?" Then as an afterthought Jessie added, "Fraidycat!"

Mabel gazed with rising fear into the swirling blackness. Then she took another step and the water swept right under her chin, even though she was standing on her tiptoes. Jessie hesitated, then stepped right up close to Mabel.

"Now, Mabel, I bet you don't dare go the rest of the way," suggested Jessie, laughing shakily. "If you aren't afraid, just go on across."

Being scared wasn't all there was to it. Mabel was very much scared. So much so that her teeth chattered. But maybe that was because the water was cold and practically in her ears. But Jessie was still daring her to go on. It was just another two steps of very deep water. If she could just see the bottom! If only the water were not quite so deep. But she didn't know what it would be like down there on those next two steps. Beyond, the bank rose steeply, with a rock partly submerged at the foot of it. If she could only reach that. Closing her eyes, she plunged.

Jessie gasped. Mabel had done it! Without a thought, Jessie closed her eyes and stepped forward too, and the next second she felt Mabel's hand pulling her up on the rock. They both stood there clinging to each other, faces puckered, tears mingling with the water dripping down their faces. Suddenly they were two best friends again, though very wet and scared.

Finally, Jessie asked, "What are we going to do now, Mabel?"

"I don't know."

"Shall we try to go back?"

Mabel glanced down at the deep water swirling about her feet and replied emphatically, "No, never!"

Jessie glanced up at the wall of slick rock beside them. "I don't think we can climb up there, do you?"

Mabel looked carefully up and down the rock wall. "I don't see how we can," she replied.

"Then what do we do?" Jessie's voice rose in fear.

Mabel leaned her head against the rough rock while the tears trickled down her face. Jessie watched her anxiously. Finally Mabel raised her head and said, "We're going to climb up, Jessie."

"We are?"

"Yes. Let's go."

"But we can't climb that bank!" Jessie protested.

"It doesn't look like it, but we are going to do it."

And they did climb that steep rocky bank. Knees and knuckles got skinned. Dirt clods and brush came loose in their hands and rained down into their tear-streaked faces. Up and up they struggled, gasping and sobbing. At last they reached the top and lay panting on the ground. Cheers rang out across the little Pilchuck as Norine, Ilene, Midget, Frances, and all the others jumped up and down.

Mabel and Jessie grinned at each other shakily. "It's just a little ways across that river, Jessie," Mabel said, "but I'd never try to go across it again."

"Nor would I." Jessie spoke soberly. "Mabel, did you pray?"

"I should say I did," Mabel admitted without hesitation. "I prayed the very best I could."

"I did too," confessed Jessie. "I don't know how to pray as well as you do, but Jesus heard us both."

"You know what I think, Jessie? I think an angel reached down from the top and pulled us right up and kept us from falling."

"I think an angel must have put his hands down for us to step onto, because I just couldn't see very many places to put my toes." Jessie's voice was soft.

"Let's thank Jesus right now, shall we?" suggested Mabel.

"Yes, and let's tell Him how sorry we are for being so foolish," added Jessie.   And let's ask Him to forgive us for being so mean to each other."

And there they knelt together on the bank of the Pilchuck and had a little talk with Jesus, all their troubles forgotten.

"Come on," laughed Jessie tremulously as she slipped her arm around her best friend's shoulder. "Let's go back across the bridge to those kids over there."

"Right, let's do that." Mabel's green eyes twinkled merrily as she slipped her arm around her very best friend's waist. Well, maybe Jessie wasn't her *very* best friend. Jesus was that, and Jessie didn't mind at all.

"I DID IT!"

THE HOME AT LAUREL Heights was an interesting place to live. The house was very nice with its large screened-in summer porch on one side. Just across from the porch was a big shed. It had an upstairs in it, but the only way to get there was by a rickety staircase built along one wall. Upstairs was rather dangerous because you might go right through the ceiling if you stepped off the two-by-fours. At the far end some boards had been nailed down, and the Williams girls soon claimed that little spot as their playhouse.

The root house, or root cellar, as some called it, was behind the shed. Root cellar was probably the better name, because it was built into the ground, with just the roof above ground. In the summertime it was a very pretty place. Why was that? Why, because wild roses grew all over it. It was cool inside the root cellar even on hot summer days. Its door was very heavy, because the space between the inside of the door and the outside of the door was packed solid with dirt. The roof had an outside and an inside too, and the space between was filled with dirt. Besides being nice and cool, the root cellar had the most delicious smells. Odors of apples and onions, of sauerkraut in a barrel, and of squash and pumpkins and potatoes all blended together with the sweet-sour, spicy smell of pickles.

The old shed was fun sometimes, and the root house was fun sometimes, but the place that was the most fun was the barn. Yes, the barn was the greatest place of all to play. It wasn't a great big barn like some people have. Oh, no! It was a little barn, covered with myrtle vine with its pretty purple flowers most of the summer. Cobwebs and dust hung from the low rafters, and everywhere was the sweet smell of hay.

The barn had three wooden stanchions for cows to put their heads through and eat. It had a big feed box just back of the mangers in the stalls. There was a small door on one side, and when you opened it you saw a closet with two old brooms hanging there and a pitchfork standing in one corner. To the left of the stanchions another door opened into a small room where newborn calves had had their home. A straight up-and-down ladder was nailed to one wall. The ladder led up to the haymow. There wasn't much hay up there, since the Williamses had no cows and no need for hay.

No, the Williamses didn't have any cows; therefore the little old barn became the perfect place for the girls and Sonny to play. Sometimes little James came out too if they promised to watch him carefully. He was only 2 years old.

The barn was just the right size for playing antony over. Or you could play badger hole alongside it. It was a good hiding place both inside and out for hide-and-seek. Oh, yes, you could have lots of fun at the little myrtle-covered barn.

Sometimes the children didn't play any games. They just sat and ate apples and talked. Now, that isn't always a good thing to do, because children can get into trouble that way. At least that is what happened one especially terrible day.

On that particular day the Williams children had been playing until they were all tired out. Maybe that was because Annie Hanson was there; and Orr; and Sonny's best friend, Henry; and Henry's big brother, Eddie. Now, maybe if Eddie hadn't been there nothing would have happened. Yes, everything might have been just like every other day if Eddie hadn't come up the hill to play with the Williams children.

You see, there was a large opening in one end of the little barn. Sometimes children get pretty big ideas even when they themselves aren't very big. Well, that was what happened with Henry's big brother, Eddie. Eddie was in the fifth grade. Norine was in the fifth grade too, but she wasn't nearly as big as Eddie. Jessie was in the third grade, Ilene was in the second grade, and Midget was in the first grade. Henry and Sonny were only 5 years old and hadn't started to school yet. Now, that great big Eddie should have known better, but, then, so should have all the children. They just shouldn't have listened to Eddie as they all sat around upstairs in the haymow.

"I'll bet I can jump out of the haymow window, but I'll bet none of you dare to do that" were the bad words that Eddie said. Now, it isn't smart to talk like that, is it? And it certainly isn't smart to dare someone to do something wrong. And taking a dare is definitely the wrong thing to do. But sometimes children forget all about right and wrong, don't they? Especially when someone says the word *dare*.

The barn didn't look large when you were outside looking at it. No, it looked pretty small compared with the house or the big old woodshed, where the girls sometimes played dolls. It didn't look far up to the haymow window. Not at all. Not when you were on the ground looking up. But when you were inside looking down out of the haymow window—well, that was altogether different. It looked very, very, very far down. Surely no one would want to jump out of anything that high. The Williams children and Annie and Henry and Orr were certain that not even Eddie would dare to jump out of that hayloft.

When Eddie said those words about jumping out of the barn window, every single child turned and looked at him, big-eyed with shock.

"Jump out of the window? Why should anyone want to do that? Why not just go down the ladder?" That's what practical Norine said. No, she wasn't impressed with all that nonsense about jumping out of the barn window.

Everyone should have listened to Norine, but there seemed to be another voice whispering suggestions too, and they weren't good ideas. Suddenly someone spoke up. Which child was it? Well, no one was just sure, but someone really did say, "Oh, Eddie, you're just saying that! You wouldn't really dare jump out of the barn window. Huh! You're just bragging!"

Maybe it was that little sound of scorn. Maybe it was that horrible word *dare*, but whatever it was, Eddie just replied, "Ho! You don't think I dare! Well, you just watch me. I can jump out of that window as easy as pie." And with a little swagger he stood up, brushed the hay off his clothes, and sauntered over to the edge of the window. All eyes watched him in silent wonder. Up he climbed onto the edge of the window opening. There he perched for an instant, then with the words "Watch this," he sailed out into space and almost instantly plopped onto the ground below.

Everyone rushed to the window. Every little head raised itself to the edge of the opening in the haymow. Every pair of eyes, blue, brown, and hazel, stared down at Eddie. Was he all right?

Eddie picked himself up, placed his hands on his hips, and announced, "There! I did it! It was easy. Now I'll bet none of you dare to do that!" His eyes gleamed in triumph as he lorded it over his awe-struck audience.

Of course no one else would dare to jump out of that barn window! Just looking down made cold shivers run up and down one's back. Of course no one would do anything so foolish! But wait a minute! Someone did dare. Yes, one of the children actually dared to jump out of that window, and it was done so quickly no one had a chance to do one thing about it.

You probably think you know who it was, don't you? You wouldn't guess Norine. No, of course not. Nor Ilene. She would never do that. And you know as well as anyone that it would never be that sweet little neighbor girl, Annie Hanson. Then who was it? Ha! You are probably thinking, Oh, I know. It was Jessie, of course. She's always getting into trouble.

Well, you are right about one thing. Jessie could manage to get into trouble without any effort at all. But it wasn't Jessie who jumped. No, the one who as quickly as a cat jumped over the windowsill and down to the ground was the tiny, fairylike girl with the big brown eyes and the dark-brown hair. Yes, it was little Midget. Who would have thought that that little whiffet would jump out of the window? No one did. Not wee little Midget. But whether you think she would or not, that is just what she did. Up and onto that two-by-four windowsill she jumped in a flash, saying, "I dare! I can do it if you can, Eddie." And out she sailed.

Stunned, the Williams children watched as Midget flew from their midst. Then they heard her laughing and saying, "There, Eddie, I told you that I could, and I did!"

Then Midget tried to stand. But something was wrong. What had happened? As she tumbled back onto the ground she turned her eyes up to her sisters and Sonny and her friends and cried, "Oh, my leg! I've hurt my leg!" Her eyes were full of pain. Tears tumbled down her cheeks. Her voice shrieked over and over, "My leg! I've hurt my leg!"

You can guess that Norine and Jessie and Ilene got down that ladder inside the barn in a great big hurry. Yes, they half tumbled, half fell down the ladder, and off to the house they raced! Mom came rushing out, gathered Midget up, and carried her home. Mom could see how badly Midget's little leg was broken.

Well, a neighbor with a car took Midget and Mom into town several miles away. Midget was patched up and put in a cast, and for a long, long time she could not walk or run or even go outside while the children played unless Daddy carried her out just to watch. Oh, how lonely and unhappy she was sometimes. But she learned a good lesson that day, and so did several other children. And that lesson was to "look before you leap." Or maybe the lesson was that you are better off if you don't let yourself be tricked by that foolish little word *dare*.

BIG BUSINESS

HELLO, HENRY," CALLED Sonny to his friend who was coming up the hill.

"Hello, Henry," his friend called back.

Now, that may seem funny to you that each called the other "Henry." But, you see, Sonny's real name was Henry, though no one but his friend ever called him that. How he wished people would call him by his real name. But, no, it was always "Sonny." He particularly wished Daddy would call him Henry. He had started calling Daddy "Dad" in hopes that Daddy would catch on that he should be called Henry.

Now, the neighbor boy, Henry, liked to come up the hill to Sonny-Henry's house to play. The visiting Henry always had a nice friendly grin, showing two missing front teeth. There was no question that he was very proud of those two spaces. Sonny wished *his* two front teeth would hurry and fall out so he could be just like Henry. Maybe then Daddy would begin to see that he was too big to be called Sonny anymore.

Sonny had been doing some thinking that morning. Real deep thinking. Daddy had been paying the girls twenty-five cents for each rick of wood they hauled to the woodshed from the woods where Daddy had cut and stacked it. Now, Sonny wouldn't mind making a little money too. He was 7 years old. That was plenty old enough to be earning money. When he approached Daddy about his plan, he found him very enthusiastic. In fact, Daddy had a beaming smile for Sonny and told him that he was very proud of a son who would be willing to help get the winter's supply of wood in the shed. Sonny blushed with pride in himself.

Now as Sonny saw Henry sauntering up the trail toward him, his mind went to work. Maybe he could start a business deal with his friend and split the profits. Or maybe Henry wouldn't want any pay. He was like that.

"Henry," said Sonny as the boy drew near, "how would you like to haul a little wood this morning? We can play horse and driver. You can be the horse some of the time, and I'll be the horse some of the time. You can be the driver some of the time, and I'll be the driver some of the time. How does that sound to you?"

"Hey, that's great, Henry," Henry replied. "Shall I be the horse first or the driver?"

"Well"—Sonny pondered the question carefully—"why don't you be the horse first."

"Sure. That suits me fine. Where's the wagon?"

"Right over there behind the woodshed," said Sonny, leading the way. He found a rope and tied it around Henry's middle, then picked up a stick lying nearby and said, "All right, Ned, let's go."

"Ned? Who's Ned?" asked Henry.

"Oh, that's you. That's the horse's name."

"Well, what's the stick for?"

"That's the whip, of course. I need a whip to make the horse go," replied Sonny. He tapped Henry lightly on the shoulder and commanded, "Giddyap, Ned."

Henry made a very willing and obedient horse, and he didn't require the use of the whip. Sonny climbed into the wagon, one leg slung carelessly over the side, and proceeded to talk to his friend, Henry. Or rather, Ned, the horse.

"Do you see Daddy over there sawing wood, Henry—I mean, Ned?"

"Sure."

"Well, I want you to drive over close to him so I can tell him we're going to haul wood now."

"All right. I like your dad," Henry—or rather, Ned—replied.

"Yes, he's a real good dad. He's going to pay me some money for helping him get the wood in."

"He is? What are you going to buy with it? Firecrackers?"

"Oh, maybe. Maybe some rockets, too. All right, Ned, stop right here. Whoa, Ned. Whoa!"

Henry stopped just as any good little horse should when his master speaks. He grinned his famous two-teeth-missing grin at Mr. Williams.

"Hello, Mr. Williams," he said.

"Hello, Henry. I see you don't have those false teeth yet."

Sonny interrupted, "Dad, we are going to haul wood for you now. Giddyap, Ned. Giddyap."

Henry plodded away toward the woodpile, Sonny jouncing along in the wagon. Upon arriving at the woodpile, Sonny jumped out. "Now I guess it's my turn to be the horse, isn't it, Henry? You can be the driver."

"Me the driver? But we're already here. What do I do now?"

"What do you do? Well, let's see. I guess you load the wagon." Sonny took his place at the head of the wagon, and Henry set to work with a will.

Sonny glanced over to where Daddy was working. But Daddy wasn't doing anything. He was just looking at Sonny and Henry. Sonny felt a little uneasy.

Henry had finished loading the wagon. Now he picked up the driver's stick and touched Sonny on the shoulder. "Giddyap, Ned. Giddyap," he called cheerfully.

"Oh, no, Henry. It's my turn to be the driver. You be Ned."

Henry looked a bit puzzled. Then he said slowly, "All right, Sonny. I like to be Ned."

When Sonny commanded, "Giddyap," Henry moved ahead a little slowly.

"You're doing fine, Ned. You really loaded this wagon well, Henry. The load is going to stay on all the way back to the woodshed."

Henry was pleased at these words of praise. When they passed Daddy, who had paused to watch them, he called, "Hello, Mr. Williams. My two front teeth are growing in. I can feel 'em."

"That's great, Henry. All good horses need teeth," replied Daddy. "Hello, Sonny," he added.

"Hello, Dad," said Sonny, but he didn't stop the wagon.

At the woodshed Henry said, "Wow, that was work. I'm glad to rest awhile."

"Here, just a minute," Sonny said. And he ran toward the house. In a few seconds he was back with a big dipper full of water. "Here you are, Ned," he said to Henry. "You've been a good horse. Now I'll be the horse and you be the driver."

"You'll be the horse? How about this load of wood?"

"Oh, the driver unloads the wood, you know."

"Sure, I guess that's the driver's job," agreed Henry, and he piled into the work, not like a tired old horse, but like a rested driver.

When the wagon was empty Sonny climbed back into it again. "OK, Ned. Time to get back to work."

Henry looked at his friend, but said nothing as he again became Ned. "Hello, Mr. Williams," he called with a big smile as they passed Sonny's dad.

"Hello, Henry. Hello, Sonny. It looks as if you have a real business going."

The wagon moved on to the pile of wood waiting for them. This time when the wagon stopped, Henry moved back and began to load wood. Sonny stepped up to Ned's place. Once he glanced up and saw Daddy, his hands crossed on his knee, just watching.

The wagon was soon loaded and Henry was pulling it along, because he was the horse again. "Hello, Mr. Williams," he called cheerily as they approached Daddy once more. "It's beginning to get hot, isn't it?"

"Hello, Henry. You're right. It is getting warm. Here, how about a drink of cold water out of my water jug."

"Sure, Mr. Williams. Thank you."

"How about you, Sonny? Do you want a drink?" asked Dad.

"No, I guess not, Dad. I'm not very thirsty." Sonny glanced at his father briefly, then stared down at his own feet.

Well, Henry and Sonny whittled down the woodpile in the woods and built the pile in the woodshed higher and higher. On each trip Henry called a cheery message to Mr. Williams. On each trip Sonny's head hung lower. Sometimes he didn't even look up. Finally the job was finished. Sonny and Henry made their way over to the place where Daddy continued to work.

"Hello, Dad. The wood is all hauled into the woodshed." Sonny grinned a kind of sickly grin.

"The job is finished, Sonny? Then I think it is time to pay up." He

reached down into his pants pocket and brought out a shiny quarter. "Here is your pay, Henry. You are a good worker."

"Oh, Mr. Williams! A whole quarter! Thank you so much." Henry beamed at Daddy.

"Henry, you are very welcome. Now you'd better run home. My watch says it's time for lunch. But maybe you don't eat lunch, since you don't have any teeth."

"Oh, Mr. Williams, I have teeth! See?" Then, turning, he ran for home. "Goodbye, Mr. Williams. Goodbye, Henry."

Sonny, fidgeting from foot to foot, stood before Daddy. Daddy picked up his saw, sprinkled a little oil on it, wiped it carefully with a rag, placed it over his shoulder, and turned toward the house. He glanced down at Sonny standing forlorn before him.

"Are you coming, Sonny?" he asked.

Sonny hesitated. "Daddy, you didn't pay me any money."

"Oh, I see. H'mmm. I didn't notice you doing any work, Sonny. It seemed to me that you were riding in the wagon or walking or just standing beside the wagon. Henry was the one I saw working. Now, I don't want to cheat anyone, Sonny, especially not you, my very own son. Tell me, did you work? I'll gladly pay you for work done. How much do I owe you? The bargain was twenty-five cents a rick, wasn't it? Just tell me how much you earned." Daddy looked squarely at Sonny.

Sonny could do nothing but squirm under Daddy's direct gaze. How much had he worked? How much had he earned? His face flushed a deep red. "I don't think I earned even one penny," he blurted. "Henry did all the work. I just want you to know I'm sorry and I'd like to work for you again. And I won't cheat next time."

"No more fast business deals?" asked Daddy.

"No, Dad. No more big business deals for me."

"Son, I'm proud to hear you say that!" And that happy, proud look was back in Daddy's eyes. His smile was warm as he placed his arm around Sonny and said, "Let's go get a few bites of Mom's good cooking and then maybe we can tackle this woodpile right here. How does that sound to you, Henry?"

Henry! Dad had called him Henry! Sonny's smile was radiant. "Right, Dad. I'll be an honest partner. You'll see!"

And he was.

DEVIL'S-
DARNING-
NEEDLE

OH, LOOK AT THIS PRETTY, lacy flying bug with its long, long body and beautiful wings! Whatever is it?'' Jessie bent over the dazzling creature to better study it as it poised daintily on a fern.

"That? Oh, be careful, Jessie! That's a devil's-darning-needle!'' May answered.

"A devil's-darning-needle? What do you mean? It's so pretty!''

"Just watch out, Jessie. There are lots and lots of nests of devil's-darning-needles living on this hill, and they are mean, let me tell you!'' Leona grinned at May and emphasized every word with a shake of her finger in Jessie's face.

"Why, what——?''

"Don't you ever dare to walk over this hill by yourself. The darning-needle will fly right up to you and sew your eyes shut, just in a flash, if you're alone. So be careful, Jessie. Don't ever walk over this hill all alone. Not unless you want your eyes sewn shut!''

"And if you tell lies they sew your mouth shut, too. Say, you don't tell lies, do you?'' May eagerly added to the story.

"No, I guess I don't.'' But suddenly Jessie wasn't sure. Sometimes—well, maybe she did tell a little lie to Ilene or Norine once in a while. Maybe— Yes, and now she was telling a lie to these girls when she said she didn't tell lies. Oh, dear! What would she do?

Mom had sent Jessie to the store to get some groceries. The store was right on the other side of this hill. How could she ever get to the store without going over the hill? She laughed a little shakily to show that she wasn't scared, not really. The other girls weren't frightened at all, but, of course, they were older than 8-year-old Jessie.

"How does one ever get to the store over the hill if he has to come alone then?" Jessie questioned doubtfully. "This is the road to the store."

"Oh, you just don't go this way. You have to take that old skid road that we passed at the foot of the hill. That leads you out to the other road that takes you to the store," Leona explained.

"The old skid road! That goes out into the deep woods, and it must be a long, long ways."

"Well, yes, maybe a mile through the woods, but that's what you have to do if you come to the store alone. Or else get your mouth sewn up. You wouldn't want that, would you?"

"No-o-o," stammered Jessie. She kept close to the other girls all the way to the store. By the time she had her few little groceries, the girls had already started back. She called to them, but it seemed that they went faster and faster. Finally, halfway up the hill, she caught up with them. They were laughing and joking.

"What's the matter, Jessie? You look scared!" said May. "Is something wrong? Did a dog chase you?"

"Oh, no," denied Jessie. "I'm not scared. I guess I just hurried fast so as to walk home with you." There, she had told a lie! Now she was really scared. She looked all around, but didn't see any devil's-darning-needles anywhere around. She heaved a huge sigh of relief.

Days sped by. And weeks hurried along. The incident of the devil's-darning-needle had almost slipped from Jessie's mind. Almost, that is, until one day a few weeks later when Mom was canning peaches and found that she was all out of jar rubbers.

"Jessie," she called, "will you go to the store for me? I need a few jar rubbers."

Devil's-darning-needles! They would be everywhere, buzzing around in the hot August sunshine. Oh, I don't dare to go, thought Jessie.

"Oh, Mom, it's so hot out. Can't Norine go instead of me?"

"Now, Jessie, it's just as hot outside for Norine as for you," replied Mom reasonably.

"Then can Norine go with me?"

"Jessie, I need Norine here to help me peel peaches. Besides, it doesn't take two girls to bring home a few boxes of jar rubbers. You hurry along now. I'll soon need them." Mom slipped a half dollar into Jessie's unwilling hand and said, "Hurry as quickly as you can, and don't lose the change."

Jessie started out, but she really didn't hurry. In fact, the closer she got to the hill, the more her feet lagged, and dragged. At the foot of the hill she stopped altogether. Should she go over the hill, with the darning-needles buzzing all around? How could she keep them from seeing her? And she was all alone, too. She couldn't think of any lies she had told, but maybe she had, and the hateful creatures would sew her mouth shut. Oh, dear! She could take the skid road through the woods, but that way was so dark and so scary, too. Which way should she take? Which way? Which way?

"I'll go through the woods," Jessie decided. "Nothing can be as bad as the darning-needles." And away she went. This time she did hurry. She ran. She saw things moving under the dark trees. She heard things in the dark trees. She heard brush crackling on first one side of her and then on the other. She heard strange chittering noises. She ran faster and faster. Her throat was dry. Her chest hurt. Her sides ached. Trembling with fright and exhaustion, she finally reached the road, and soon she was at the store. She bought the jar rubbers, and then it was time to return home.

What to do? Back through those scary woods or over the hill? It was hard to decide. Jessie didn't want to go either way. Reluctantly she chose the hill. As she neared the danger point she began to hurry. Faster and faster and faster her feet flew. To the top of the hill, over the hill, to the bottom of the hill. Her throat burned and she was gulping for breath, but she had made it! Not a sign of the hateful insects. With a sigh of relief she continued the walk home.

And then it happened! All her hurrying had been for nothing. For nothing at all, because right there, right close to the screen door, sat a devil's-darning-needle on the lilac bush! A big, beautiful creature with a long, long body and gorgeous lacy wings. How would she ever get by it and into the house? Fright rose within her and almost choked her. "Mom," she called, "come here quick! Hurry!"

Mom paused in her work. What was wrong? Jessie's panicky voice startled her. She dashed to the door and followed her daughter's glance to the beautiful creature on the lilac bush.

"Oh, Jessie, isn't it beautiful? Don't frighten it. It's so lovely!"

"But what is it, Mom?" Jessie's voice had lost some of its fear.

"It's a dragonfly, one of the most beautiful of God's flying insects. Be careful, Jessie. Don't frighten it. Just step up as close as you can and look at it. See its very large head and the enormous eyes. And notice its wings all crisscrossed with bars. That makes them strong, even though they look so fragile. Notice its interesting head. Its jaws are heavy and horny, probably so that it can bite off tough grasses. It has such a beautiful, long, straight bluish-black body, and those delicate bluish wings. And to think that you found it and wanted to show it to me! But you sounded frightened, Jessie. Were you?"

Jessie looked at her mother shamefacedly. "Yes, I was."

"Why, dear?"

"Well, because I sometimes tell lies and I thought it would sew my lips together. That's what some of the big girls told me."

"Oh, my funny little Jessie." Mom laughed as she drew her frightened little girl into her arms. "Don't you know that God made these beautiful creatures for us to enjoy, because He loves us so much? He made them for His pleasure and for ours. And they have nothing to do with our lies or anything else like that. If we tell lies we just go to God and confess to Him. He is our good and loving friend. He forgives us gladly. Don't be afraid of His beautiful creatures. Just look at them carefully and find out all you can about them. The more you know of His creatures, the more you will know of God's love. That's the important thing, isn't it?"

Jessie smiled at her mother. How silly to believe all the scary stories of the big girls. They were just teasing her. She would learn to know God's beautiful creatures because they would teach her about His love, just like Mom said. And, thought Jessie, one of the very best things about God is that He gives little children such wonderful mothers! And Jessie was right, don't you think?

WHAT NEXT?

HEY, MOM, LOOK WHAT Ilene has," called Norine one Sunday evening as she dragged her sister into the kitchen, where Mom was ironing. "What's the matter with her, Mom? She's all speckled!"

"Speckled! What are you talking about?" Mom pulled Ilene to her.

"Right there, Mom. See around her lips, and see, she even has speckles inside her mouth!"

Mom looked inside Ilene's mouth. Bluish-white spots. She pushed Ilene's nightgown down off her shoulders. She looked at Ilene's chest. She shook her head. She looked at Ilene's back, then shook her head some more. It was quite obvious that Mom was pretty upset about the rash that was just beginning to appear on Ilene's chest and back. And she was pretty dismayed about the spots on the inside of Ilene's mouth.

"Ilene, I do believe you have the measles," she said. "Tomorrow we will call the doctor to be sure, but all those specks and spots look like measles to me. Now I suggest that you jump into bed. No school for you tomorrow."

"Oh, Ilene, you are lucky!" exclaimed Norine. "Just think, you can just stay home and play with your dolls and draw pictures and things like that, while we have to go to school and study and do arithmetic." Norine was trying to cheer Ilene a bit because she was looking pretty scared. Measles sounded like a terrible disease.

"All of you get to bed," commanded Mom, "or no one will be ready for school or even breakfast in the morning." She turned, her eyes searching the room. "Where's Midget?" she inquired. "Why isn't she here ready for bed?"

The children looked at one another blankly. Where was Midget?

"I think she must be here in the kitchen," said Norine. "She wasn't in the other room with us."

Mom called, "Midget? Where are you, Midget?"

"I'm right here, Mommy," quavered a tiny voice.

"Midget, what on earth are you doing behind that cookstove? You should be all ready for bed," Mom scolded.

"I am so cold, Mommy. No, I think I'm so hot. I feel funny, Mommy, and my throat is awfully sore. My head feels funny too," Midget whimpered.

"Here, let's take a look at you," ordered Mom. "Open your mouth!"

Midget opened her mouth. Um-h'm! Bluish-white spots. Mom undid Midget's dress. Sure enough, there was that same fine red rash as Ilene had. Mom just kept shaking her head and saying things like: "Yes, just like Ilene. It must be measles." Then she would add, "But where did they get it?" No one could answer that.

"Well, Midget," said Mom, "a nice warm bath for you and into bed you go."

"No school for you tomorrow, Midget," consoled Ilene. "We get to stay home and play dolls and draw pictures."

"I don't want to draw pictures and play dolls," stated Midget.

"But won't it be fun just to stay home?" persisted Ilene.

"No!"

"Well, what do you want to do then?"

"Just go to bed and be sick," Midget replied.

"Be sick? Who wants to be sick?" was Ilene's scornful reply. But by morning she felt as bad as Midget. Dolls didn't interest either little girl. Neither did coloring books, nor playing store. They both wanted to be left alone and just be sick.

Now, Jessie rose early because she thought she would be going to school. Was she ever surprised when Mom told her that she and Norine and Sonny would all have to stay home from school.

"Why do I have to stay home? I'm not sick!" wailed Jessie.

"No one in this family goes to school until we find out what kind of bug is around," said Mom firmly.

"I don't have any bugs," insisted Jessie. "I want to go to school."

"But you aren't going, Jessie. Not until the doctor comes and tells us what is wrong with Ilene and Midget."

A new fear rose in Jessie's thoughts. "Mom, how long is it until Valentine's Day? We just have to be in school on Valentine's Day! Our room is having a party."

"It's more than a week away. Maybe you will all be able to be back in school by then, but if not, you will just have to make the best of it," soothed Mom.

"But I'm not sick," stormed Jessie.

But by evening Jessie wasn't sure about that. Her throat hurt. Her eyes watered and she was sneezing. She was hot and shivery and her head ached. Norine was acting as though she wasn't feeling well either. She wasn't reading any books, and if Norine wasn't reading a book she must be sick. Yes, by evening both Norine and Jessie were definitely not feeling well. They both crawled into bed about the same time and didn't talk to each other. They didn't talk to anyone. They didn't want to do anything but lie quietly and be sick. The doctor came and told Mom that all four girls had the measles, and that no one could come to visit them and no one in the house could go visit anyone until he gave permission.

Oh, dear! How about Valentine's Day? Well, if you have had those real honest-and-truly measles, you don't think about much of anything, certainly not valentines. Poor Ilene was so sick that she even thought she saw spiders creeping and crawling everywhere. When Mom would pretend to kill one spider, Ilene would think she saw another one. Mom just very nearly ran her legs off rushing from one fussy girl to another. Then Sonny and James got the measles too. Oh, dear! Such an awful time.

The days crept by in that house of sickness. The days galloped by at school. Then came Valentine's Day. The schoolchildren didn't forget their speckled friends in the Williams home. No, indeed! Annie Hanson came trudging through the grove and the meadow right up to the back door with a shoe box almost filled with valentines. There were some for Norine, some for Jessie, some for Ilene, some for Midget, and some for Sonny. And can you imagine James's surprise when he received two valentines also? Everyone seemed to feel better right away, and they had so much fun looking at all the pretty cards. Some had bluebirds and flowers. Some folded down so that the whole valentine looked like a beautiful flower garden with plump little cherubs holding arrows aimed at hearts. And nearly all had lacy edges and ribbons. Oh, they were really beautiful.

Valentine's Day passed. Another week went by. The children were all feeling better, but when they begged to go back to school, Mom just kept saying No.

"You may go back to school when the doctor says you may," said Mom, and she meant it. There was no use teasing to go to school or anything else if Mom said No.

Then the doctor came.

"Where are all my sick patients?" he joked. "Do you think I should come miles out here into the country to see well people?"

Well people! That sounded pretty good.

"When can we go back to school?" Midget asked the jolly doctor.

"Now, don't get in a hurry, little miss," replied the doctor. "This is Thursday. If everyone is feeling well by Monday you can all go back then."

Of course, everyone felt just great. Ilene and Midget and Sonny had been feeling well for days. Norine was coming along pretty well, and so were Jessie and James.

Sunday came. Just to prove that the world was a very lovely place, a beautiful, gleaming sun came out and smiled down on the world. All around, daffodils and crocuses were pushing their way through the ground. Birds were beginning to twitter in the branches. The Williams children pressed their faces against the windowpane and beamed. They talked excitedly of school and their friends. Finally Ilene asked, "Mom, would it be all right if we went outside to play?"

Now, it's almost certain that having the children outside would be a tremendous relief to Mom. You know that four sick girls and two small sick boys and Baby Louis could get to be quite a noisy burden for a mother who has so very, very many things to do. So Mom looked at that nice, beautiful sunshiny day and thought, That's an excellent idea!

"If you bundle up well and don't tear around and get all hot and tired, it will probably be all right," she agreed.

Each child solemnly promised to be very good. And if you had been cooped up inside a house for more than a month, you would have certainly agreed to be very good, wouldn't you? Oh, yes, indeed. The children bundled up in sweaters, coats, and hats, and down the steps they tripped, out into the beautiful March sunshine! They had such a good time. All the old familiar places seemed new again. They explored the shed and the playhouse. They tested the swing. They were all so happy. That is, for a while.

Then suddenly that noisy little Jessie seemed to just wilt. That's right. Jessie didn't feel so well. Not anymore. Her eyes began watering. She got cold. Yes, she was definitely cold, even though the sun was shining nice and warm. "I'm going inside," she told the other children.

"Going inside? Why, we just got out!" said Ilene.

"I'm not going in until the Fourth of July," stated Midget.

But Jessie just shook her head and went into the house.

"Why, Jessie, what's the matter?" asked Mom anxiously. "Don't you feel well?" She stroked her daughter's flushed face. It was hot. "Dear, I think you had better go right back to bed." Jessie needed no urging.

The next day all the Williams children except Jessie returned to school. Jessie stayed in bed. Her temperature was high. Her eyes watered so much that damp puddles formed all over her pillow. Oh, she was a sick little girl. Mom was frightened. Again she called the doctor, and he made the long trip to the Williams place.

"Keep Jessie in bed," the doctor instructed Mom. "I'll put something in her eyes and I want you to put more in several times each day. Be sure to keep her eyes covered all the time. I'll be back in a couple of days."

The something that he put in Jessie's eyes was dark brown, and somehow seemed to stick her eyelids together. After a few days she began to feel better, but still the dark gooey stuff was put into her eyes. Now, when you are sick that isn't so bad, but when you begin to feel good you want to do something. You want to read something or paint something. You want to do anything but just lie in bed all day long and do nothing. Jessie began to wonder if she had to have her eyes bandaged forever. Mom and Dad hoped that she wouldn't be blind, and Jessie certainly hoped so too.

The days passed slowly. Jessie's birthday was on the fifteenth of March, and she began to worry about that. "What about my birthday, Mom? Do I have to wear these bandages then?" she fretted.

"Let's not worry about it, Jessie. If you are still in bed, we'll have a birthday cake with candles anyway. How will that be?" Mom consoled.

And that is just what they did. Jessie still had bandages on her eyes, but she did get one quick peek at that cake. It had ten candles on it. She blew the candles out and hoped her wish would soon come true. And what did she wish? Why, that she could soon go to school again, of course.

Now, a birthday cake isn't the only good part of having a birthday, is it? There are presents too. Jessie stole a quick peek at each present. Just one, that's all. The first gift was a tiny beaded purse from Annie Hanson. Good, sweet, kind little Annie, who was adopted. She was one of Jessie's best friends. Oh, how beautiful that little purse was! Jessie just loved it!

The second present was a book from Mom and Dad. It was titled *Uncle Ben's Cobblestones*. Jessie knew that she would treasure that book a long, long time. It was full of interesting stories about everyday things, even salt. Yes, there was a story about salt and how some little children and older people too would have a piece of salt to lick on rather than sugar. Can you imagine that?

The third present was perhaps the most exciting gift of all. No, not that it was any nicer. Nor was it more expensive. Do you know why it was the most exciting gift of all? Because Jessie had never seen the person who gave it to her. No, Jessie had never seen or even heard about the little girl who gave her that third gift. Isn't that strange? The gift was a book of all the *Our Little Friend* children's papers for one whole year. Yes, fifty-two *Our Little Friend* papers tied together with blue yarn. Each little paper looked as if it were brand-new.

Who gave Jessie these papers, this lovely gift? They were from a little girl named Alice. Alice was Mabel's cousin, and, of course, you remember that Mabel was Jessie's best friend. Why did Alice send such a nice gift to Jessie? Well, perhaps it was because she was a Christian who had heard that Jessie had the measles and that her eyes were affected by the disease. Maybe she had heard that Jessie might never see again. Perhaps Jesus whispered to Alice that she could be a real missionary by sharing her Sabbath school papers. And since she was a Christian girl, she wanted to help Jesus in whatever way she could.

Jessie loved that little girl whom she had never seen. Of course she did. Wouldn't you have? And Jessie didn't go blind. In a few weeks she was perfectly all right and out playing with the children again. But she treasured each story in that book of *Our Little Friend* papers. Jessie resolved in her heart to love and serve Jesus by helping other people just as Alice had done.

You know, we have a Friend whom we have never seen face to face. He continually gives us good gifts, hundreds of them every single day. All because He loves us. And the best way to show that unseen Friend that we love Him too is by loving and sharing with others.

ANSWERED PRAYER

IT WAS A SPECIAL DAY, YES, a very special day. Mr. Edwards was driving from his home far away to the Williams place in Laurel Heights. What was so important about that? Well, Mr. Edwards was going to take the older Williams children over to his new place. They were going to stay several days with the Edwardses, and best of all, they were going to get to go to Sabbath school. You see, there was no Sabbath school to attend in Laurel Heights. Of course, there was that Sunday school at the top of the hill on the way to the store, but hardly any children ever went there. Now the Williams children could go to Sabbath school with Mabel and Fran.

On the way to the Edwards place the children sang songs and counted all the cars on the road and named them if they could. Ford, Star, Hupmobile, Dodge . . . The car jogged and jounced over the rutted gravel road, its canvas sides flapping in the breeze. The Williams family didn't own a car, so you know how much fun the children had rolling along at fifteen to twenty miles an hour.

Sabbath was a beautiful day. All the younger children, from the little tiny folks to the big ones about 12 years old, had Sabbath school in the back room of the church. That back room was the church school on school days. No, it certainly wasn't a very large schoolroom, that was sure. Not at all like the big two-room schoolhouse in Laurel Heights.

A lovely little lady whom everyone called Auntie took charge of the children's Sabbath school. They sang songs, then had prayer. Then the teacher told them all to stand and sing "Hear the Pennies Dropping." Everyone did, and they all marched around and dropped a penny or whatever offering they had into the offering box.

Ilene looked at Jessie. Jessie looked at Ilene. None of the Williams children had an offering.

"Jessie," Ilene whispered, "what do we do now? We don't have any pennies. Do we get up and march around with the others?"

"I don't know," Jessie whispered back. "I guess if you don't have any pennies you just sit still." She sounded doubtful. "No, maybe we wouldn't look so funny if we got up and marched around with the others. We can pretend we are dropping in pennies, I guess," she concluded.

Ilene gasped. "Jessie, that wouldn't be right! Besides, you can hear pennies dropping."

Both girls squirmed in their seats until Mabel quietly slipped her hand over into Jessie's lap and dropped four pennies into it. "Give one to Ilene," she whispered, "and one to Norine and one to Midget."

Jessie looked at Mabel with a smile of relief. Mabel had only one penny left, but she didn't seem to mind at all.

When all the children were back in their places Auntie asked, "Did you bring a Bible to Sabbath school today? You older children are big enough to find our memory verse in your own Bible, aren't you?"

All the children nodded their heads, their faces beaming. All, that is, but Norine and Ilene and Jessie and Midget. They didn't have a Bible. Not one of the Williams children owned a Bible. They had never looked up a memory verse in the Bible. Their heads hung low and their faces didn't beam. Oh, dear, no!

"Do you have someone or something you would like to pray for today?" asked Auntie. Nearly all the children had something that they wanted to talk to Jesus about, and suddenly Ilene did too, but she was too shy to say what it was.

Ilene knew how to pray. Of course she did. She had been saying her prayers as long as she could remember. Now she resolved that before she came to the "God bless" part of her prayer, she was going to quietly ask Jesus for a Bible, a Bible of her very own.

And that is just what she did. And she kept on asking. Every night she prayed, "Dear Jesus, please send me a Bible."

Sometimes prayers are answered with a surprise, but Ilene's wasn't. Or maybe it was, because, you see, the Williams children had a special person named Aunt Rose who came to see them once in a while. She would usually bring a box for the children. Sometimes it was used clothing. Sometimes there were real treasures in the box of things. For instance, once there were some tiny little pill bottles. What fun were they? Why, if you went to the beach you could look for very small seashells. You could put a different kind in each bottle and tie the bottles all together with pink ribbon and hang them over your dresser. You could then show them to all your playmates when they came over.

Aunt Rose would tuck bits of lace, pieces of velvet, and beautiful ribbons into the box. And knowing all this, you can be sure that everyone was happy when she came one day and brought her box of surprises along.

Eagerly the children opened the box.

"Oh, this is mine!" exclaimed Norine. "It's a book!" And she pulled out *The Story of Peter Cottontail*. She soon lost interest in everything else. Another book, *Cuffy, the Bear*, went to Jessie, who liked to read almost as much as Norine. Then there were bits of this and that grabbed by eager little hands. Ilene just sat there taking nothing, but she was not at all unhappy.

"Ilene, don't you want anything at all?" asked Midget.

"Sure I do," replied Ilene, "but you haven't come to my gift yet. It's in there."

More things came out of the box. Ilene looked at each article as it was removed.

"Ilene, if you don't take something pretty soon, there'll not be one thing left for you. Here, wouldn't you like this wide piece of lace?" asked Norine.

"My present is in the box. You just haven't come to it yet," responded Ilene. "It's there somewhere."

One more item, then another, and another. Soon the box was empty. Ilene hadn't claimed a thing.

"Here, Ilene, I'll share with you," said Jessie. All the others offered to share too, but Ilene just shook her head.

"My present is in there," she insisted stubbornly.

Oh, how sorry Jessie and Norine and all the children felt for Ilene! She hadn't asked for a thing, and now the box was empty. What could they do?

"Let me look," said Ilene. She slid up to the big box and looked inside. Sure enough, it was empty. Ilene slipped her hand down inside that empty box. She felt all around it, almost as if there might be something there that her eyes couldn't see. But it seemed to be completely empty, all right. Why couldn't she see that it was empty? Couldn't she believe what her own two eyes and her own two hands told her? Ilene was a funny girl, that much was sure!

Ilene was still feeling around the box. Finally she lifted out some crumpled-up tissue paper and newspaper. And guess what? Yes, out of that paper tumbled a book. A Bible? Of course. It was only a small, old, well-worn New Testament, but it was a Bible. Where did it come from? Not even Aunt Rose knew how that little New Testament came to be at the bottom of the box. But Ilene knew. God had heard her prayer and answered it just as she knew He would.

Yes, God heard Ilene and God hears us. The Bible says that "before they call, I will answer; and while they are yet speaking, I will hear." * Yes, before Ilene even prayed God knew her need, and while she was praying He was preparing a box and a Bible. And Ilene believed God even when it looked as if He weren't paying any attention to her prayer.

God hears and answers your prayers too when you ask for gifts that will bless you and others. Just try Him and see.

---

* Isa. 65:24.

WHAT'S THAT NOISE?

SH-H-H, JESSIE, BE QUIET, can't you?'' Norine cautioned.

"Well, what do you see?" whispered Jessie.

"I can't see a thing."

"You must see something. After all, we can see the light shining through up here, so we should see *something* down there." Jessie spoke firmly.

"No, I can't see a single thing."

"Move over and let me take a peek. I'll bet I can see something," commanded Jessie.

"Maybe *you* can see something, but I can't." Norine slid back away from the crack where the light shone through. Jessie took her place. Carefully she peered through that one crack. Nothing. She twisted her head this way. Nothing at all. She twisted her head that way. Still she could see absolutely nothing.

"You're right, Norine," she whispered. "I can't see a thing either. But there has to be some way we can find out."

"I'll tell you what," returned Norine, "why don't you just go downstairs and get a drink of water? You can take a good, quick look around and find out what is going on."

"Too late," said Jessie. "I tried that already."

"You did?" Norine whispered, surprised. "You never told me."

"That's because it didn't work."

"Why not? What happened?"

"I guess Mom must have heard me creeping down the stairs, because she met me at the door."

"Did she tell you to go back upstairs and get into bed?"

"Well, something like that. She brought me a drink, but she closed the stairway door before she went after it," Jessie giggled lightly.

"And you didn't see anything at all?"

"No, not a single thing. Dad is doing all that pounding and sawing in the kitchen, anyway. I couldn't see way out there from the stairs, you know," explained Jessie.

Both girls crept back into bed, but their whispering continued.

"You know, I never thought a thing about it when this pounding and sawing started early in November," said Jessie.

"I didn't either except that we were sent to bed with the birds every evening," Norine grumbled, because she wanted to stay up and read. "Who can go to sleep so early, anyway?"

"I don't know," said Jessie. "Dad must be making Christmas presents, but for *two months?* He could have built a house in that length of time."

"You must remember that he has only evenings to work here. But still, that's a lot of hours."

"And where does he hide whatever it is he's making? I've peeked everywhere I can think of, but haven't found a thing, not even a scrap of lumber in the morning. How can everything disappear so completely?" Jessie shook her head.

Now, you know there is something exciting about a mystery, and it's even more exciting to be able to solve the mystery. But when you can't find a single clue—well, that gets frustrating. Of course, neither Norine nor Jessie would have thought of teasing Mom or Dad to find out what was going on. No, indeed. None of the Williams children ever teased Mom or Dad, or whined or pouted or nagged. It may not have been forbidden, but it just wasn't done. Not in that family.

Days rolled by. Norine peeked into closets. Jessie snooped in cupboards. They explored all the dark corners of the old shed, where the playhouse was. Nothing. Nothing at all. They moved everything in the summer porch. They looked under beds and in the barn, upstairs and down. They even looked in the root cellar. Each time they just shook their heads. How could Dad pound and saw every night and the mystery disappear into thin air each day?

Then suddenly the pounding stopped. The house became quiet again at night. The crack of light in the floor didn't gleam very long after the children went to bed. Was Dad finished? And where had he put whatever he had made? Whatever it was, it was simply not anywhere. And, of course, that's impossible, isn't it?

A few days before Christmas, Dad and the children went out searching for a Christmas tree. The perfect tree was easy to find, and each child soon had one picked out. Dad looked each of them over carefully, and the very best one was chopped down and hauled into the house. Dad fixed a stand for it, and Mom and the children made popcorn strings and paper chains and decorated it. It was beautiful.

Now it was time to put the presents under the tree. Norine and Jessie had hemstitched handkerchiefs and made other little gifts for the smaller children. They wrapped them and placed them under the tree. And that was all. There wasn't another present under that tree. Not a thing from Mom or Dad. That was odd! How about all the hammering and pounding?

"I don't believe we are going to get anything from Mom and Dad," whispered Norine to Jessie.

"Maybe they can't afford gifts this year," said Jessie. "Dad's been out of work so much."

"Mom says that with so many mouths to feed it's a wonder we do as well as we do," Norine said soberly.

"Well, I think we'll get something. Mom and Dad will find a way," Jessie said loyally.

"Maybe we will get oranges. That's good enough for me," Norine whispered, and with that thought in mind, both girls turned over and went to sleep.

Christmas Eve came. The house was full of the good smell of fresh bread and wild blackberry pie. All the children were scrubbed clean. They had the eager, expectant look that little children have at Christmas time.

"Dad, where are the presents?" asked Sonny.

"Presents? What presents?" Dad teased.

"Why, our Christmas presents," Sonny explained patiently. "It's Christmas. Where are our presents?"

"H'mmm. You're right, Sonny. I don't see a sign of a present. Now I wonder why?" Dad pretended that he was very surprised to see nothing

under the tree. Jessie and Norine knew he was still teasing. "Well, maybe by morning old Santa Claus will have come down the chimney and left you something."

And then Sonny knew that Dad was joking. He knew that Santa Claus was really Dad or Mom. They were the ones who put the gifts under the tree. "You are fooling me!" he scoffed.

"Well, you run along to bed now, Sonny. And you girls too. I'll bet you will find an orange under the tree in the morning."

"An orange sounds good to me, Dad," said Norine. "I know you don't have much money this year. We don't mind at all, do we, Jessie?"

"Of course not," said Jessie, fondly putting her arm around her wonderful dad's neck.

"Well, I do have something, even if it isn't money," replied Dad.

Oh, he was going to tell them! Now they would know what the pounding and hammering and sawing were all about.

"Oh, what? What do you have, even though you don't have money?" inquired Norine breathlessly.

Dad looked thoughtfully at his daughters, then hugged each one close to him. "I have a very fine family," he stated simply, "and two lovely big girls who help with the household burdens. I'm proud of you. Now off to bed. It will soon be Christmas Day, and we'll have wild blackberry pie!"

That wasn't the answer that Norine and Jessie expected. Dad hadn't told them the secret, but somehow that no longer mattered. Each girl felt that she had received a special blessing, and sleep came easily to them that night.

Then morning came. Christmas morning. Ilene and Midget crept silently out of bed and tiptoed down the stairs and into the living room. Their eyes grew wide, then wider. But they uttered not a word. No, not one word. Each girl's mouth formed a round O, but no sound came out. Then they did a strange thing. They turned and silently sped back upstairs and into the older girls' room.

"Jessie! Norine!" Ilene and Midget shook the older girls awake. "It's Christmas morning."

"Come on, get up," urged Ilene. "Come and see!"

"You can never guess, never! Not in a million years," whispered Midget excitedly.

Now you might as well know that sometimes Jessie and Norine didn't like to be wakened so early in the morning, but this morning they were out in a flash and stumbling down the stairs. There in the living room stood Sonny and James, staring with round, shiny eyes first at their presents, then at the girls.

Suddenly everyone began talking at once.

"This has my name on it, and so does this!" squealed Norine.

"Where's mine?" shouted Midget above the confusion.

"Here's mine, and your name is on these two presents!" shrieked Jessie.

The hushed silence had become a thing of the past as the children found their gifts. Yes, *gifts*. Each child had two. The boys each had a wagon and a train engine. Sonny's wagon was large enough for him to ride in or to haul wood in. James's was a little smaller. Both the wagons and the engines were painted bright colors and were just perfect.

Norine had a kitchen queen. Do you know what that is? It's partly like a table and partly like a cupboard. Down below, it has a door that swings out, and there inside is a bin for flour. Another door swings out, and there is a bin for sugar. Then there are drawers for silverware and lids and dish towels. There is a place for pots and pans and cake pans and pie tins. Like Mom's big kitchen queen, Norine's had a breadboard and a rolling pin. And Dad had made every bit by hand!

Jessie's gifts were a library table and a most beautiful dresser with a mirror that could tip forward or back. Ilene's and Midget's gifts were just alike. Each had a bed and a cedar chest.

And that furniture wasn't small doll furniture. No indeed. It was LARGE. The dresser was about two feet tall, and the kitchen queen and table were at least a foot and a half high. The beds were large enough for big dolls. Oh, those Christmas presents were the most wonderful gifts in the world!

"So this is what the pounding was all about!" exclaimed Jessie.

"No wonder it took Dad so long. Just think, all these pieces of furniture to be sawed, put together, stained, and finished." Norine shook her head wonderingly. "I'll bet Mom did the staining and finishing," she added.

"I guess they love us a lot. That's why they did all this," spoke Midget wisely.

And who could deny that? Yes, surely Mom and Dad loved those children a lot. Every minute they were sawing, every minute they were pounding, every minute they were painting, they were loving their children. No, there wasn't much money in the Williams family, but that didn't stop a loving father and mother from giving gifts. Not at all.

Do you remember that verse in the Bible that says that men, though they are evil, know how to give good gifts to their children, but how much more will our loving Father in heaven give good gifts to His children here?* Notice that the verse says how much *more* God is willing to give good gifts to His children. Even more than Dad and Mom Williams did for their children? More than that hard work every evening for so long? Yes, more than that. It's hard to believe, but God loves us even more than that. He really does.

---

* Matt. 7:11.

DADDY IS COMING

HURRY, ILENE! AREN'T you ready yet?'' Midget's voice was a little impatient.

"Coming, Midget,'' replied Ilene, joining the group.

It was Friday evening, almost time for the sun to sink behind the tall trees to the west of the Williams home in Cedarhome. The Williams family had moved from their Laurel Heights home over to where the Edwards family lived. There the children could attend church school and go to Sabbath school every Sabbath. Norine was about 12 now, or maybe 13, and Jessie was almost two years younger. Ilene was about 10, and Midget was 9. Then there were the boys— Henry, who used to be called Sonny, James, Louis, and the baby, Gene. Well, what a family! Just like the old woman who lived in a shoe, all right.

Friday evening was special in the Williams family now, just as it had been in the Edwards family for many years. How much better it was that Jessie and Mabel and Ilene and Fran and Midget could go to school and to Sabbath school together, and begin Sabbath in the same way. And that way is with Sabbath worship, of course.

But every Friday evening, just after worship, the Williams children did a strange thing. Yes, I'm quite sure that you would think it very odd. After the last bath was taken, the last hair ribbon was in place, the last prayer said, the Williams children put on sweaters and coats and caps. Yes, that's right. Now, after Friday evening worship you probably hop into pajamas and get all ready for bed, don't you? So you see, the Williams children did do a very strange thing, didn't they? After they were all ready, the children walked down the lane to the stand where farmers set their cans of milk for the hauler to pick up each morning.

When the children reached the milk stand, the older ones would help the younger ones up onto the stand, then they would climb up too. There they would huddle, happily waiting, waiting.

Now, why would all these children be doing this when it was beginning to grow dark? Sometimes it was cold out there, too, even though the stand had a roof on it and a wall in the back and on two sides. Why would these children make this strange trip in the dark and in the cold?

When the children got up into the milk stand, they would all turn their faces toward the west. They would look up to the top of their hill and on to the top of the next hill where the trees parted and the road ran through and on and on. Yes, they kept looking to the west, way up the road to that opening between the trees. But why?

The children sang songs or told stories or guessed riddles while they waited, but they always kept their eyes toward that far-off opening between the trees. And by and by they would be rewarded. Yes, a small, faint light would appear on the crest of the second hill. Just a tiny speck, it seemed to waver a few seconds, then disappear. But the children didn't look away. No, they kept their eyes on that opening between the trees, watching breathlessly, and then—there it was. It reappeared, not as a single dim speck, but as two lights. Hushed silence. No more songs. Each child craned forward to watch, the older children clasping the smaller ones to keep them from falling.

On and on came the lights, growing larger and larger and brighter and brighter. The children's eyes never left those two lights coming ever closer. Then the car drew abreast of them, and passed right on by, just like that!

As it disappeared into the night the children relaxed with a disappointed sigh. The little ones climbed off the laps of the older children. Talking resumed until someone called, "Look, I see another one!"

Instantly all were at attention again. Silent. Waiting. The single distant light wavered a few seconds high on the second hill, lowered, then disappeared, only to reappear shortly as two lights. As each moment passed, tension again mounted. Silence. Hope. Disappointment as that car too drew abreast, then disappeared.

On some evenings this was repeated several times. First hope, then disappointment. But never did the children give up and drift back to the house. No, not even once. Because they knew that finally that little speck of a light growing brighter and brighter would stop right beside the milk stand. Yes, it always happened. Every time. So the children never gave up. And neither would you have if you had been there.

"Hey, look! Here comes another," someone called. Sure enough. First the tiny, faraway light, then the two lights gradually growing closer and closer. But this time as the car came real close, it went slower and slower. Then it stopped right in front of all those children on the milk stand. Someone called from inside the car, "Hey, Jim, are those your chickens roosting there in that milk stand?" The Williams children laughed. They had heard similar words week after week for a long time.

And Dad would reply, "I believe so, but maybe I'd better count and see."

But, of course, he never had time to count anything, because hardly had the car stopped than all those children hopped down out of that milk stand and swarmed around him. Yes, it was Friday, and Dad would be home until Sunday night, when he had to return again to the logging camp way up in the hills.

As the laughing, shouting children surrounded their father, he would give one child his empty lunch pail to carry. Another was handed a small suitcase with his clothing in it. One might be given Daddy's raincoat. But one fortunate child, a different one each time, was given a special brown paper bag. Whoever carried that held it very carefully all the way to the house. Now Daddy's hands were empty. Sometimes he swung little Louis up onto his shoulders, or if Louis couldn't come out that evening, he would extend a hand to a child on each side of him. And away up the lane they would all head for the house, hopping and skipping and laughing. Dad was home!

Once inside, the precious paper bag was handed to Mom, who opened it and let all the children choose a candy bar from inside. And I guess you know that candy was a real treat for those children.

Dad would tease his family by saying that they waited for him only so that they could have candy bars, but that wasn't so at all. How do we know? Why, because Dad brought candy bars home only on payday, that's why. But the children waited for him every week, not just on payday weekends. They waited and watched for their dad because they loved him so much and wanted him home with them.

Now, maybe you have already thought of something else. Have you? Of course. Jesus is coming back soon. Are you all clean and waiting and watching for Him? When He comes He is going to bring gifts for each of us too, isn't He? But are you waiting for the gifts? No, of course not. We want Jesus Himself, don't we?

STUBBORN AS A MULE

JESSIE STEPPED CAU-
tiously up to Billy. She had the harness straps all fixed over his head, the bit in his mouth, the straps properly placed over his back; now she had only to reach under the horse's wide stomach and grab the strap from the other side and she would have him harnessed and ready to go.

Earlier, Mom had asked her to run over to the Edwardses' to see whether they could borrow Billy and the big sled to help them haul wood. "Sure. Help yourself," said Mr. Edwards. "He's up there by the barn. Just grab that short rope hanging in back of the barn door. Slip that around his neck and take him into his stall. You know where the harness is. Just help yourself."

Well! Just help herself. Should she? Jessie had helped Mabel harness the horse lots of times, but she had never done it alone. She pretty well knew where all the straps belonged, but she always managed to be busy with something else when it came time to reach under Billy to get that particular belly strap. Mabel always did that. No way did Jessie want to get her head down there and get it kicked off by one of Billy's great big feet. Now here she was being told to just help herself. In other words, she was supposed to harness that horse all alone.

"Whoa, Billy. That's a nice horsy," she said shakily. "Now stand still. That's a good old horse."

Cautiously Jessie placed a hand on the broad back, then lowered her head to peek under and find the strap on the other side. Suddenly Billy's skin rippled under her hand, and back she jumped in fright. Billy turned his head and gazed at her curiously. Jessie's heart beat fast, but she bravely stepped up to the horse again.

"There now. Nice Billy. I won't hurt you." Again Jessie placed her hand on his back and with her other just started to reach for that strap again when Billy gave a loud snort. Back jumped Jessie, sweating and trembling.

Billy, you wretched old beast, thought Jessie to herself, why won't you stand still and behave yourself? But aloud she tried to speak calmly. "Whoa, Billy. That's a good old horse. Please just stand still now while I finish getting you harnessed."

Again Billy turned his head inquiringly and looked at the girl. Was it scorn in his eyes? Certainly there was no fear there. Maybe it was pity. Well, anyway, thought Jessie, I'll harness you yet even if it kills me! If she just didn't have to get so close to Billy with her head down! Down so near to those big feet! Jessie had to admit that she wasn't too fond of Billy or of any other creature his size, for that matter. It would be great to be like Mabel and just step up to a full-grown horse and never blink an eye. Jessie knew she wasn't as brave as Mabel, who didn't seem to be afraid of anything.

"All right, Billy. Let's get this harnessing done. You stand there like a nice fellow and I'll just get that strap. And, remember, I'm not afraid of you. No, sir!"

Again Jessie stepped up to the horse. She gazed at his left hind leg. Was it moving? Was it? Sure enough, up it came and back Jessie flew. It was really a false alarm, because Billy barely lifted his foot off the floor and then placed it back down. Jessie was exasperated with Billy and with herself.

"What on earth are you doing?"

Jessie swung around. There stood Mabel in the doorway.

"What does it look like I'm doing?" Jessie exploded. "I'm harnessing this horse so that Mom and I can haul wood."

"Well, don't keep jumping around like that. Don't you know that that makes Billy nervous?" scolded Mabel.

"Makes Billy nervous!" fumed Jessie. "Those big feet of his make me nervous, that's what!"

"Do you mean that Billy tried to kick you?" asked Mabel in astonishment.

"Well—— Come on, why don't you help me finish harnessing this horse? Here, you get that strap that goes under his belly."

Mabel just looked at Jessie. She stepped up to Billy and, without a word, grabbed that belly strap and had it hooked in seconds. Then she led the horse out and hitched him to the sled.

"I can do the rest now," Jessie said, and away she started with Billy. Away down the lane. But something was wrong. The horse walked half a dozen feet and stopped. Just stopped and drooped his head as if he were dead tired.

"Giddyap, Billy. Let's get going," called Jessie. Billy started up with a jerk, walked a few feet, and stopped. He heaved and puffed as if he were hauling a tremendous load.

"Billy! Giddyap! Quit your poking along!" commanded Mabel. Billy turned and looked back at her, then away he trotted. No more stopping. He knew Mabel and he knew she meant business. He moved right along until he rounded a curve, then that stubborn horse stopped, every bit of him expressing the despair of a tired, worn-out animal.

That going a few feet and stopping kept up all afternoon, whether the sled was empty or full. Either way Billy was just completely exhausted, and who would be so cruel as to work such a pitiful old horse? Yes, every few steps he would have to stop. He slumped and sagged and sighed, if horses do such a thing as sigh. Anyway, judging by Billy's looks and actions, he was tired out. According to Jessie, he was something else again—stubborn as a mule!

Finally the wood was hauled. Needless to say, Jessie was actually a lot more tired than that lazy, stubborn horse. So was Mom. The patience of both of them was worn pretty thin, too. It was with relief that Mom and Jessie viewed their completed wood-hauling job, grateful that they no longer had to put up with Billy.

"There, that's done," sighed Mom. "Take him home, Jessie, and I hope we don't have to use him for a long, long time."

Jessie turned the horse toward the Edwards place and called, "Giddyap, Billy. You can head for home now."

Billy glanced back at Jessie once more. Could he believe his ears? No more wood hauling? Suddenly his youth returned. Up went his head. Every muscle in his large body was alert and ready to travel. At Jessie's second giddyap he was off like a shot. Jessie had no time to jump on the sled. All she could do was run this way and that way, dodging the swaying sled and trying to dodge the brush along the roadside. She didn't dare let go of the reins because she had borrowed the horse and must return him and the sled unharmed.

Finally they arrived at the barn door. Jessie was torn, scratched, miserable, and angry; Billy, eager, alive, and having a glorious time.

Mabel came running toward her friend and her horse. "Jessie! What on earth happened?" she cried.

"Well, if you want to know the truth, this horse is crazy. He's so tired when he knows there is work to do that he can't even pick up his feet, but he practically leaves the earth and takes to the skies when the work is done! And just look at me!"

Mabel had been looking, and suddenly she doubled over, laughing. Jessie was a sight to behold as she stood there, sore, dirty, and angry. "You and your dumb old horse!" Jessie exclaimed bitterly. "I'd rather carry every log from the woods myself with my own two hands than fool with that horrid beast!"

Mabel only laughed louder. "Never mind," she finally gasped. "We will teach him a lesson. We'll go horseback riding, and then he'll wish he had behaved."

Now, maybe that was a good idea as far as the horse was concerned, but Jessie was not quite so sure. After all, it was she who was carrying all the battle scars. Reluctantly she agreed. If they could teach Billy a lesson, a real good, stiff lesson, it would be worth it.

They both mounted the horse, Mabel in front, Jessie in back. Now, if you are in front you have the reins to hang onto. Also the mane. You can see where you are going, too, which helps a lot. But sitting in the back is quite different.

Mabel knew her horse, and without a doubt, Billy knew Mabel. He might be stubborn, but he knew that Mabel was in charge when she spoke. "Giddyap, Billy, let's get moving," Mabel said firmly. And they moved. In and around crooked corners, over low stumps and logs, this way and that, she guided the horse. Jessie bounced along, clutching Mabel desperately as back and forth she slid on Billy's rolling back.

"Whoa, Billy!" Jessie shrieked, but Billy ignored her. After all, who was that redheaded kid anyway? "Mabel! Make him stop! Whoa, Billy! Stop, you dumb old horse!" But Billy galloped on. Jessie's head jerked this way and that as on they hurried over the craziest race track ever devised.

"Mabel, stop him! Stop right now! I've had enough horseback riding. Stop him, I say!" Jessie blubbered.

Now, Billy respected Mabel's voice, and Mabel respected Jessie's voice. Mabel slowed Billy down and they finally stopped.

"All right, Mabel. Thanks for the ride. I'll get off right here right now," stated Jessie firmly. "I've battled Billy all day. Now if you want to show him a thing or two, you go right ahead. I prefer walking." She began to dismount, but Mabel laid a restraining hand on her arm.

"Oh, Jessie," she begged, "don't give up so easily. We have to teach Billy a lesson."

"Well, what about me? What lesson are you trying to teach me?" snorted Jessie.

Mabel laughed. "I guess yours is a lesson in patience," she replied. "You know, Jessie," she continued, "horses are smart. They know when a person is afraid of them. You must never act afraid. You must speak firmly. The horse must sense that you are in charge. Sometimes you may even have to give the horse a good slap to let him know you are boss. Now, why don't we change places. You call the commands to him like you really mean it. You have to learn, you know."

Jessie was unconvinced. "I've been commanding him all afternoon, and I've meant every word of it. That old rascal would pant and puff for about two steps and then stop. No, he won't budge for me. I know that already."

"Yes, you've commanded him, and you've meant it, but you've never *sounded* as though you meant it. You've sounded scared. You've got to let him know that you are the boss. You have to be stronger than he is. Come on, Jessie. It won't hurt to try."

"All right," Jessie reluctantly agreed. Mabel swung off the horse and Jessie scooted forward. Then Mabel swung up behind.

"Now, remember what I've told you. Be firm. Be fearless."

"All right. I'll do just that," Jessie replied, and without pausing she yelled, "Giddyap there, Billy, and I mean it!"

Wow! Billy got the message, but Mabel wasn't quite ready for the takeoff. You remember that when one sits in back he doesn't have the reins to hang onto, and he doesn't have the horse's mane or the horse's neck to cling to. And if one doesn't watch out, disaster may overtake him. Mabel hadn't even bothered to hang on to Jessie. When Jessie boomed, "Giddyap there!" and whacked Billy sharply on the neck, the horse sprinted forward like lightning unleashed. At that moment Mabel somehow left his back, doing a somersault on her way down.

Jessie had all she could do to hang on to the reins as she bounced crazily along. She glanced back, horrified, to see Mabel draped ungracefully over a huckleberry bush, her hair trailing in the dust.

"Whoa, Billy," Jessie screamed. She must have sounded very much in charge, for Billy stopped instantly, or maybe even quicker. At any rate, it was much too quick for Jessie, who went flying over his neck and plummeted to the ground eight feet in front of the horse.

When Jessie recovered her breath, she lifted her head carefully, wonderingly, and gazed back at Mabel, who was untangling herself from the huckleberry twigs. Each gazed at the other wordlessly, then slowly they grinned. Then their eyes turned to Billy. There he stood between them, quivering, eyes rolling. Both girls burst out laughing.

Billy stood there, head erect, nostrils flaring, sides heaving. In spite of his wild eyes, he still managed to look the part of wounded dignity. He gazed sadly at Mabel, or so it seemed to her. A horse betrayed. He looked at Jessie, then with a snort, a toss of his head, and a flip of his tail, he turned and trotted back to the barn.

"That looks like the end of lesson number one!" laughed Jessie. "But you have to admit he obeyed my commands when I really meant them."

"You are right," agreed Mabel. "All you have to do is show him you are in charge, and believe me, you did do that all right." The two friends laughed as they brushed dirt off their clothes and headed back toward the house.

And, boys and girls, that is not only the best way to speak to horses but how we should respond when temptations come to us. We have to show Satan that he cannot control us. We must be able to say, "Get thee behind me, Satan," and really mean it. What can he do to us? Nothing, really, if Jesus is with us. When Jesus is in charge, we can win every time.